IT'S IN HIS KISS

A RIVER WINERY NOVEL

JEN TALTY

HAVE WE GOT A STORY FOR YOU!

Dear Readers:

Welcome to Candlewood Falls!

Each Candlewood Falls story stands alone. However, the end of one story doesn't mean the end of your favorite characters. They can show up in any Candlewood Falls book at any time.

Candlewood Falls is a unique world of connected stories by different authors whose characters, business, and events appear in each others' stories.

Think of Candlewood Falls as a literary soap opera.

Be sure to check out the the other authors and discover which other books include your favorite characters.

Happy reading!

Stacey Wilk & K.M Fawcett & Jen Talty

PRAISE FOR JEN TALTY

"*Deadly Secrets* is the best of romance and suspense in one hot read!" *NYT Bestselling Author Jennifer Probst*

"A charming setting and a steamy couple heat up the pages in a suspenseful story I couldn't put down!" *NY Times and USA today Bestselling Author Donna Grant*

"Jen Talty's books will grab your attention and pull you into a world of relatable characters, strong personalities, humor, and believable storylines. You'll laugh, you'll cry, and you'll rush to get the next book she releases!" Natalie Ann USA Today Bestselling Author

"I positively loved *In Two Weeks*, and highly recommend it. The writing is wonderful, the story is fantastic, and the characters will keep you coming back for more. I can't wait to get my hands on future installments of the NYS Troopers series." *Long and Short Reviews*

"*In Two Weeks* hooks the reader from page one. This is a fast paced story where the development of the romance grabs you emotionally and the suspense keeps you sitting on the edge of your chair. Great characters, great writing, and a believable plot that can be a warning to all of us." *Desiree Holt, USA Today Bestseller*

"*Dark Water* delivers an engaging portrait of wounded hearts as the memorable characters take you on a healing journey of love. A mysterious death brings danger and intrigue into the drama, while sultry passions brew into a believable plot that melts the reader's heart. Jen Talty pens an entertaining romance that grips the heart as the colorful and dangerous story unfolds into a chilling ending." *Night Owl Reviews*

"This is not the typical love story, nor is it the typical mystery. The characters are well rounded and interesting." *You Gotta Read Reviews*

"*Murder in Paradise Bay* is a fast-paced romantic thriller with plenty of twists and turns to keep you guessing until the end. You won't want to miss this one..." *USA Today bestselling author Janice Maynard*

PROLOGUE
CHABLIS

Seventeen years ago…

Chablis River stared at her older brother by a year with her mouth hanging open. She couldn't believe the words that were tumbling out of his mouth. Malbec had told her what he planned on doing, but she absolutely didn't believe he'd go through with it.

Not after what she'd told him she planned on doing. She'd made a commitment to this family, which meant she'd have to make the hardest decision of her life. Whatever she chose, it would change her and she'd have to live with that for the rest of her life.

"I'm serious, Mom," Malbec said.

"So am I." Her mother folded her arms across her

chest and leaned against the counter in the gift shop of the family winery.

Weezer River was not the kind of woman you argued with and won. Weezer ran a tight ship both at the winery and with her children. She had high expectations and failure wasn't an option. A lot of people viewed Weezer as cold and harsh. But Chablis admired and respected her mom. She aspired to be like her in business, though perhaps not so much in her demeanor.

Chablis stood behind the counter and held her breath. She placed her hand over her stomach. She'd made the appointment this morning. She had time before it was too late to have a choice.

This couldn't be happening.

She'd graduated from college one month ago. Dax had shown up with roses and a smile and she'd caved to his charm. They had one beautiful night.

But the morning brought the same old fight and Chablis did what she always did.

She chose family.

She chose her career.

But Dax hadn't really given her a choice because he was going back to Buffalo regardless. He wanted her to follow his dreams, which meant giving up hers and that wasn't fair.

Nothing about their situation was fair.

And neither was this.

She'd come home, as she'd been expected to do, so

she could help her brother run the family business even though part of her did want to follow Dax to Western, New York. She'd done her best not to eat, breathe, and sleep his hockey career. Her focus had to be the family wines. She'd promised her parents.

She'd promised her siblings.

And it's what she loved to do.

"If you don't tell me, I'm taking that offer in Napa Valley." Malbec held his stance five paces away.

"You wouldn't dare," her mother said. "Besides, who in their right mind would hire you? You're a River, for crying out loud."

"It's a bona fide offer and if you don't tell me the secret, I'm flying out on Friday."

"You've got to be fucking kidding me," Chablis said. "That's in two days."

"Watch that tongue of yours, young lady." Her mother arched a brow.

Chablis rolled her eyes. "You can't up and leave. This is you and me together. We're a team. And a good one." Four weeks ago she'd told the man she loved more than anything that she would never leave Candlewood Falls or her family's business. While they lay naked in bed, she looked him square in the eye and told him he wasn't as important as the River Winery.

Cement filled her gut.

Had she made the biggest mistake of her life?

"You're right. You can't," her mother said. "If he

3

leaves, none of you are running this place. I'll keep doing it."

"Mom. Now you're being childish," Malbec said. "Merlot is in college and when he's done, he can come help Chablis. Besides, she's just as good as me, if not better in some ways."

"She's nowhere near as good as you," her mother said, staring her in the eye. "You better make him stay." Her mother pushed from the counter and stomped through the main room. She paused at the front door and turned. "Because if he doesn't, your days being in the wine-making room alone are over. You're not ready. You don't have the skills and frankly, the deal was always Malbec, you, and Merlot. Without Malbec, you might as well do something else."

"Mother," Malbec said sternly. "That was uncalled for and totally false."

Chablis stood there with her heart bleeding on the floor. Her mother had called her a failure. She tried to tell herself that her mom was trying to make Malbec stay. That this was just the way her mom operated. She'd said things she didn't mean; however, she'd never been this cruel before.

"Not really," her mom said. "You needed to apprentice after me when you graduated. Chablis is green. She has a lot to learn. She's not ready and without you, she never will be. This is my winery and we run it my way. So, stay and you don't have to worry about what happens to Chablis."

"Tell me the secret and I'll stay," Malbec said.

"That secret stays buried with your grandfather." Her mother stepped through the door and disappeared.

"Don't you dare do this to me." Chablis climbed over the counter. She poked her brother dead center in the chest. "I lost the love of my life because of this winery and—"

"You should have followed him," Malbec said. "I told you that four years ago and I told you that when you told me you were pregnant."

"Shhhhhh. I don't want anyone to know."

"You need to tell him."

"He's made it perfectly clear we're done."

"No. You did," Malbec said. "You're the one who asked him to settle for something less than his dream while you settle for less."

"I was in high school when Dax went away the first time. Mom and Dad controlled that. Besides, Dax was actually scared of them and encouraged me to stay at school." She sucked in a quick breath and let it out in a huff. "I never told you, but I had my bags packed the end of my sophomore year when he signed his first professional hockey contract. I was ready to stick my middle finger up at this place, but I stayed. For you. For this family. We both know she's serious about not giving the winery to any of us if you leave."

"She'll cave eventually."

"Please. Have you met our mother?" Chablis fought

the tears that burned her eyes. "You've really looked at flights, haven't you?"

"I have one booked." Malbec squeezed her shoulder. "I can't do this with Mom anymore. And to be fair, neither can you. Go find Dax. Tell him how you feel and for God's sake, tell him about the baby. Don't do this because it's what's expected. Do it because it's what you love."

"But you're leaving and you've always loved making wine. The rest of us, it's kind of what we do, but it's not a passion."

Malbec smiled. "I'm not leaving the wine business. I'm just getting away from the Weezer. Maybe if you do too, she'll figure out we're not kids anymore and we can make our own decisions."

The thought of going against her mother's wishes was both utterly terrifying and exhilarating at the same time.

Perhaps a road trip to Buffalo, New York, was just what she needed.

Dax

Since the age of four, Dax Fabion had dreamed of being in the National Hockey League and today not only had he dressed for his first game, but he'd stepped out on the ice and scored his first goal as a professional hockey player.

Damn that felt good.

And then he scored a second and that felt fucking great.

He couldn't wipe the smile off his face if he tried.

No one thought he'd get more than a shift. Maybe two with the exception of power plays. However, after only two and a half minutes and putting his team in the lead, the coaches shifted the lines and he was rotated in as if he'd started the game.

At twenty-three, his hard work had paid off. He'd proved he had what it took to skate with the best of the best.

"Yo, Dax. Over here," Greg, one of his new team-mates, called from across the bar. Actually, Greg wasn't just any teammate. He was the captain and one of the greatest hockey players that ever played. "You're sitting with me tonight."

A few other teammates chanted his name as he meandered through the crowd. Perfect strangers cheered.

Dax couldn't even describe what he was feeling during the game, much less right now. He'd paid his dues between prep school, juniors, and division one college hockey. Signing with a team at twenty-two and playing the farm team was one thing. Being called up his second year and playing in the opening game had been nothing short of a miracle.

His heart beat so fast he could barely feel it. Getting to this place was hard. Staying here was going to be the real test of his grit.

"What are you drinking?" Greg asked.

"Vodka-soda. Double."

Greg waved the bartender over and ordered a round of drinks, plus a bunch of shots. "You were fucking amazing tonight. I knew you'd be an asset to this team."

"Thanks. I appreciate that." Dax took his drink and sipped. A few of the girls at the end of the bar smiled and waved. The bar was filled with mostly family and friends of the team, but there were a few overzealous fans who wouldn't mind being on the arm of a studly hockey player.

Dax gave both the once-over. Neither were his type. Hell. He hadn't been able to find someone that interested him since he left Candlewood Falls.

He'd been doing his best to forget about Chablis River. It had been three years since he'd last seen her and two since she'd called.

Her family was more important to her than him and who was he to fault her for that?

Except he did.

Her mother was controlling and her dad, while he mostly understood, agreed with Weezer. Chablis was to tow the party line. She couldn't make a single decision for herself. Her parents had picked her college and her degree. Her life had been planned out and there wasn't room for Dax in it.

Not unless he was willing to give up his dreams.

Never going to happen.

Not many people had the talent—and determination—to make it in the NHL. But Dax had both in spades.

Not that he was big on bragging. He tried to be humble about his accomplishments. And there were younger players who were just as good as him. He wasn't the only one. But he was damn good, and the league knew it and rewarded him with a contract with one of his favorite teams.

"Where'd that sister of yours go?" Greg slapped him on the shoulder.

Dax laughed. "She's not twenty-one and she and her friends are going to some frat party on campus."

"Oh. That sounds like trouble," Greg said. "Sorry your parents couldn't come. But I'm sure they are proud of you. When I met them a couple of weeks ago, they seemed like good people."

"They are the best."

"They think you are and I have to agree," Greg said. "Before we know it, you'll be starting and I'll be retiring."

Everyone had heard the rumors about Greg leaving the sport at the end of the season. And he made jokes about it left and right. However, the other chatter around the water cooler was the fact that the organization was looking for a couple new superstars and Dax was the name that kept rolling off everyone's tongue. He'd done his best to ignore all the rumors. He couldn't focus on what he couldn't control.

But now that he was on the roster, he needed to stay there.

"I will hate to see you leave the sport, but I won't mind taking your spot," Dax said.

"Spoken like a true player." Greg raised his drink before downing the shot in one gulp. "But it's not me this year that needs to be worried." He pointed a finger across the room. "On the ice we're a big happy family. Off, some of us don't get along. Watch your back with those three. They don't want you here because you're a threat to them."

One of the men at the table was the person who ended up sitting most of the game because of Dax and he'd since given him the cold shoulder. Dax understood jealousy. He'd been dealing with it most of his career. When he'd been in high school and made varsity as an eighth grader, not only did the kids treat him poorly, but so did some of the parents. Travel hockey and prep school were a little better since he wasn't always the best on the ice. He always tried to be humble about his talents, even when the articles came about him being one of the greatest college players and when he'd been one of the hottest draft picks.

Everyone on this team had worked hard to get where they were, and he knew that one day some hotshot twenty-something would come in and take his place. That's how this worked. He couldn't be number one forever.

But he'd milk it as long as he could.

"I'm not going to apologize for playing my best," Dax said. "But I'm also not going to be a dick about it."

"That's good, but they will," Greg said. "Keep your head down and don't engage in their bullshit. You're going to have some good games this year, but you're also going to have some shit ones too. Don't let those bad moments and games get under your skin. Those guys over there let everything bother them and that's why they have one foot out the door, and not just this organization. Their careers are going to be over soon. But you have the skills to do this for a long time." Greg tapped his temple. "Do you have the mentality to do it?"

"I do," Dax said with the kind of confidence his pee wee major coach had instilled in him. He told him to never be cocky. To never walk around as if he were better than everyone because he wasn't. But to understand that he had a gift and there was nothing wrong with knowing he was talented.

"Good." Greg nodded. "Now, I'm going to give you another piece of advice."

"Okay."

"See all these ladies? They all want of piece of you.

But watch out for crazy eyes. They will eat you alive, take your money, and leave you for dead." Greg leaned forward. "My first wife I met in a bar like this and it was a shit show and I didn't learn my lesson with my second wife."

"And what about your current wife?" Dax dared to ask.

The bartender pushed another round of shots in front of them. "He met me in this bar," she said. "I'm the owner and I'm the queen of crazy eyes." She looked over her shoulder. "The one wearing the pink shirt with the girls hanging out. She's been with half the team. She likes new blood. Stay the hell away from her. She's needy and doesn't let go easily. She's not worth the fuck."

Dax choked.

"My wife is blunt," Greg said. "However, you're young and you're a little uptight. It's time to let loose and maybe get laid."

"I concur," his wife said. "The cute quiet girl over there in the corner with Mugs and his wife, she's a real sweetheart. She too likes hockey players, but is a little more discriminate and word has it she's hot for you."

"Let's make the introductions."

Before Dax could protest, Greg raced across the bar and grabbed the young lady. The last time Dax had been with a woman had been Chablis and she'd taken his heart and ripped it to shreds.

Maybe mindless sex would help him get over her.

"Dax, this is Traci."

"It's nice to meet you." Dax took her hand and kissed it.

She had a sweet smile, nice figure, and kind blue eyes. Definitely not crazy.

"Can I buy you a drink?" he asked.

"I'd love a white wine," she said.

"I'll leave you two alone," Greg said.

Dax didn't pay much attention to where Greg went. Instead, he focused his gaze on the pretty woman perched on the bar stool. "So, are you from Buffalo?"

"Born and raised," Traci said. "You had a good game today. I was impressed."

"Thanks."

She leaned closer, pressing her bare leg against his, making it obvious what she wanted. Who was he to deny her?

He tapped his finger on her leg to test the waters. "What do you do?"

"I'm an assistant manager at a boutique." She brought her wineglass to her pink lips and sipped while pressing her forearms against her breasts, creating more cleavage.

If he had to guess her age, he'd say she was a good ten years older, but all he wanted to do was get lost in someone or something.

"What kind of store?"

"Sporting goods, so if you need a new stick, I might be able to help out."

Dax laughed, but it was cut short when a familiar face strolled through the crowd of people. "No fucking way." He set his drink on the table and wiped his eyes. He had to be seeing things. Chablis had made her choice clear when she said she'd never leave Candlewood Falls, her family business, or her mother.

"What's the matter?"

"I think I have a visitor," he said, wondering if Chablis saw the game. He was also curious how long she'd been standing there watching.

He dropped his arm over Traci.

"Who is she? Because she looks kind of angry."

"An old friend from home," he said.

She had no right to be pissed off. He'd come to her with his tail between his legs. He wanted to find a way to make things work between them. He was tired of missing her, but she couldn't tell her mother what she really wanted wasn't the winery.

He cupped Traci's chin and kissed her lips. He tried to make it passionate, but it fell short. At least on his part. "Will you excuse me?"

"Are you going to go talk with her?"

"I need to. I won't be too long." He kissed her one more time so she knew he wasn't going to ditch her for Chablis, then slipped from the bar stool.

Chablis scurried away.

"Hey," he said. "Wait."

"I'm sorry. I shouldn't have come."

"But you did." He curled his fingers around her

forearm. Electricity shot across his skin like a lightning bolt. He took a step back.

"I just wanted to tell you nice game."

"You were in the stands?" He stood awkwardly in the middle of the bar. He tried to swallow but his throat was too dry. He wished he'd brought his drink with him.

"Not great seats, but it was so great to see you out there and hear the fans chanting your name." She smiled. "And to watch you score your first NHL goal. I remember when we used to talk about what that might be like."

He tapped the center of his chest. "A million times better than we imagined." Except she wasn't waiting for him outside the locker room to celebrate.

"Did your parents or sisters make it?"

"Camila was here because she goes to University of Buffalo, but she's not twenty-one yet and she has a big exam. It's nice living here because I get to see her a lot."

"I'm sure."

"But my parents had to stay back in New Jersey with Nova. She has a big gymnastic meet she couldn't miss."

"I've heard she's a rock star on the vault."

"She's got a few colleges looking at her," Dax said.

A long silence built between them, but he no idea what to say. He glanced over his shoulder. Traci waved with a big smile.

So not his type.

"Can we go outside?" She glanced over her shoulder. "It's kind of loud and crowded in here. I feel like everyone is staring at me."

"There's a back patio. It will be a little cold, but at least there isn't any snow. But I need to let my girlfriend know."

"Girlfriend?" Chablis raised a brow.

"It's new." He turned on his heel and took the ten steps back to the bar. "I'm sorry, but I have to step outside with her." He lifted his drink and chugged. "Promise me you won't go away?"

"Kiss me like you mean it and I'll stay right here."

He took her into his arms and took her mouth in what he hoped looked like the kind of wet, sloppy kiss a man gave a woman he wanted. "Be right back." He patted her bottom. When he turned, his heart landed in the pit of his gut.

Chablis had a look of disgust plastered on her face.

He blew out a puff of air. He knew he was acting like a child. He had no excuse other than his feelings were hurt. He placed his hand on her lower back and guided her toward the door. A million things ran through his mind as to why she might have made the trip.

None of them were good.

Once outside, he stuffed his hands in his pockets. It was unseasonably warm for October, but still, fifty degrees was a bit chilly. Besides, if he didn't do something with his hands, he might try to take her into his arms and kiss her because he missed those damn lips.

He'd been with other women since they broke up, but no one compared to Chablis. He told himself it was because she was his first, and maybe that was true; however, standing in the cold under the moon, he knew he still loved her.

"You should have called me and told me you were coming. I might have been able to get you a better ticket."

"I didn't want to affect your mental game." She climbed up on the picnic table and tucked her hands between her thighs. "I'd read in the paper that you might be getting a lot of ice time and I didn't want to add to the stress, considering the last time we saw each other things didn't end well."

"No, they didn't." He wasn't sure he could do this again. Walking away from her last month had been the hardest thing he'd ever done. "I have to ask. Why are you here? Is everyone okay?"

She let out a short breath. "Malbec went off the rails."

"What does that mean?" He sat next to her, but kept a safe distance. Touching her wouldn't be smart.

"He moved to Napa Valley."

"Shit. Seriously?" Dax jerked his head. That was huge news. "What happened and how did Weezer take that?"

"It's all over that stupid secret that my mom won't

give up and she's being her usual self. She's not letting me step into Malbec's spot. I did everything she asked and now just because Malbec's having a late rebellion, I don't get to run the wine-making. She's forcing me to take a back seat. I didn't spend all this time in college to run a cash register or to be used as a pawn in a game between her and my brother."

"That's fucked up." He scooted closer and wrapped his arm around her and squeezed. He'd known her family his entire life. Malbec had been one of his best friends growing up. He'd spent a lot of time at the River house between being Malbec's buddy and Chablis' boyfriend. Dax had been lucky because both Weezer and Carter liked him, only they were never going to approve of his choice to chase his dream. They quickly made their position clear and Chablis chose them, not him.

Twice, she made that choice and he swore he'd never allow himself to get sucked back in because she'd always choose family.

Always.

"I'm sorry that your mom isn't respecting all that you've done and isn't giving you the respect you deserve, but what does it have to do with me?"

"I told my mother that if she's not going to give the wine-making responsibility to me, as planned, then I'm going to do exactly what Malbec did."

"You didn't?"

"Oh. I did. And Merlot got into it."

"I don't believe it," Dax said. "I can see Malbec growing a pair and standing up to the Weezer, but Merlot? Never."

"You heard about what happened to Caleb, right?"

"I've spoken to Caleb a few times," Dax said.

"Now that Malbec is gone, and I'm leaving, Merlot is going to switch his major to criminal justice."

"Good for him." Dax put a little space between them. He couldn't trust himself to be this close to her. But he'd never allow himself to be part of her world again. "Why are you here, Chablis?"

"Don't you get it? I left the winery. I'm leaving Candlewood Falls."

He pushed from the table. His heart hit his stomach like a brick. "You'll never leave."

"My bags are packed." She stood and placed her hands on his shoulders. "I know you're seeing someone new, though I can't believe it's that girl."

"Hey. You don't know her, so don't judge her."

"Sorry, but one month ago you were in my bed," Chablis said.

"And you kicked me out." Dax folded his arms. "Are you telling me you came to Buffalo to tell me you want me back?"

"Yes," she said. "And that I'm willing to do it your way. I'm not sure what I'm going to do for a living at this point and there is another thing we need to discuss but—"

"Go home, Chablis," Dax said. "We have nothing to

discuss. I'm not doing this with you again. You will never leave Candlewood Falls or the bosom of your mother, and I'm never going back. Never. Not even when I retire from this sport. You and I were high school sweethearts. That's it. Nothing more. Nothing less. We're over. For good. Now, I need to get back to my current girlfriend before she gets the wrong impression."

Dax was going to have to tell Traci that tonight wasn't going to happen. He couldn't use her that way and hopefully she'd understand. He'd focus on getting his emotions straight and keeping his hockey career on the right track.

Chablis

Chablis took the information the nurse handed her and waited for Malbec. She sat in the wheelchair in the recovery room and stared down the corridor. Her hands trembled. Tears burned her eyes.

Malbec came into view.

When he caught her gaze, he picked up the pace.

She sucked in a deep breath and let it out slowly.

"Hey. How are you holding up?" Malbec knelt and took her hands. "Are you in pain?"

"No. At least not physical."

He wrapped his arms around her and gave her a big brotherly hug.

"Thanks for coming back for this," she whispered.

"I wasn't going to let you go through this alone." He kissed her forehead. "Mom thinks I'm having second thoughts. But I'm not. I'm sorry that she's being so hard on you and that Dax wouldn't hear you out."

"I hurt him to the point he couldn't forgive me, and I know you think I should have told him about the baby, but I didn't want him to take me back out of obligation. It was obvious that he was done with me."

"I know. I went and saw him this week."

Chablis tilted her head. "What? Why would you do that?"

"You know I would have supported your decision regardless. This is your body and there are no judgments here. This is the right decision for you, so me going to see him has nothing to do with your choice not to have a child right now."

"Thank you for saying that, but seriously, I don't appreciate you going to see him," she said. "But now that I know, what happened? What did he say?"

"We didn't speak. I went to the bar you told me about after the game and I saw him with some girl who was hanging all over him. He's changed. He's not the same guy who used to sleep over so he could steal kisses with you."

Chablis knew she loved Dax the first time he kissed

her when she'd been fourteen years old. "Mom always said you'd know you were in love because it was in his kiss."

"You'll find love again." Malbec smiled.

Maybe he was right; however, her bigger problem was finding a career and she had the perfect solution. "Before you take me home, I've got one more favor to ask."

"What's that?"

"I want you to pull something out of a hat for me."

"Excuse me?" Malbec looked at her like she had ten heads.

"I put ten different careers that I could go into in this baseball cap." She reached into her large bag. "I want a witness to keep me accountable."

"What kind of jobs are in here?" Malbec asked.

"Things you would never expect me to do like a police officer, a flight attendant—"

"You hate flying."

She laughed. "My favorite is working the alpaca farm."

"Right, because you love those creatures."

Holding the hat up, she gave it a good shake. "Pick a good one."

"Okay." He flicked a few papers around before finding one. He unfolded it, holding it up to his face. "Oh, my. I will enjoy watching you try to do this one."

"What is it?"

He turned the piece of paper around and she read the word scribbled on it.

Firefighter.

"Guess I better figure out how to become one of those." Her life certainly wasn't turning out how she thought it would, but for the first time she was in complete control.

1

CHABLIS

hablis put on a smile as Serena Tillman approached. "Good afternoon," she said. "How can I help you?"

"My son and I are here to see Dax Fabion. Do you know when he's coming?" She glanced at her watch. "According to your mom, he should be here by now." Serena's husband used to play with Dax at Candlewood Falls Prep School and they weren't close. As a matter of fact, Toby barely tolerated Dax off or on the ice.

Dax always tried to be kind and include Toby, but Toby made it impossible.

And what made it worse was Toby's father who was always yelling at Toby in the stands or belittling him when he got off the ice. Toby's dad would either tell him he was the best one out there and he got robbed or that he better step it up because he played like shit. It was so sad to watch.

5

Even sadder now that Serena, who wasn't very likable in high school, had married Toby and they'd produced a son, who now played hockey.

Chablis' heart hit her stomach like a whale reentering the ocean after a magnificent breach. She knew she was going to have to deal with all of this sooner or later. She was just hoping it would be later.

Some commotion at the front of the store caught her attention. "Looks like he's here now."

Serena took her teenage son by the collar and dragged him toward the door while Chablis turned on her heel and headed for a place where she could take a breath.

She gripped the counter in the back room behind the gift shop where they stored wines for tastings and breathed deeply. She thought she was ready for this day, but she wasn't. Far from it.

Seeing him again brought every emotion, both good and bad, she'd ever had for Dax to the surface.

"Hey, are you okay?" Malbec asked.

She knew her brother meant well by following her, but she really didn't want to talk about it. "Yeah. I'm fine."

"I call bullshit on that." He squeezed her shoulder. "Between Eliza Jane and Riesling being pregnant and Dax coming back to town, I'd say you're having a moment."

"Then let me have it in peace." She turned, knowing

Malbec wasn't going anywhere. While she was close to all her siblings, she and Malbec shared a bond that she didn't have with anyone else, and that was only because he'd kept her secret.

From everyone.

They were the only two people who knew what she'd done. She had no regrets. She'd made the right decision. There was no way she could have raised a child on her own. She wasn't Riesling. She didn't have the courage or the tenacity that her sister had.

Besides, if she'd had the baby, Dax would have given up his career. She knew that about him. He was an honorable man and he would have come home to take care of her and his child and he would have resented both of them for it.

"I knew I was going to end up seeing him today. I've practiced a million different responses in my head. I don't know why I'm stressing over this so much."

"Do I really need to say this to you again? You basically went through that time in your life alone."

"I had you," Chablis said.

"That's funny considering the entire time you blamed me for so many things because I left," Malbec said. "Besides, all I did was hold your hand for a couple of days. You had to go through all the emotions by yourself. You never told anyone but me. You dove into your career and pretended things were fine when they weren't."

"I'm sorry about how I treated you after you left. You didn't deserve my wrath. I did and do understand why you left. But you have to understand that I needed to do what I did to get through it." Chablis focused her attention on becoming the best firefighter she could be and giving back to her community. She loved her job. Still did. And now that Malbec and Merlot were back in Candlewood Falls, she switched gears and it was time for them to take over at the River Winery.

Things had come full circle.

So why the fuck did Dax have to come back and stir everything up, reminding her of all the things she didn't have?

"All that did was help you bury it deep in your soul," Malbec said. "I remember when Ashling was born. You struggled with that. And now that two more babies are on their way and Dax is back, it's bringing it all up again."

"I'm at peace with my decision. I'm happy for you and I'm ecstatic for Riesling and Trey. I really am."

"We know that." Malbec pulled up a stool and patted it. He made his way to one of the wine racks and pulled down a bottle of Pinot. He opened it and poured two glasses. "What's going on with you right now has nothing to do with us. I get that you're at peace with the decision you made but—"

"I'm glad you can recognize that."

"You're not with the fact that you never told Dax."

"I can't deny that." She lifted the glass, checking out the color of the wine. It amazed her how much she'd remembered about the wine-making process, especially since she'd tried to forget about that part of her life. She'd even stopped drinking vino for a few years because all it did was remind her of Dax. "I can't believe it's been seventeen years since I've last talked to him."

"That's a long time," Malbec said.

"I can't believe he retired. He's still at the top of his game. I bet he has a few more years left." She swirled her wine before taking a slow sip. Damn, her family knew how to make the good stuff.

"Did you watch his press conference?"

She nodded. He'd been so poised and professional in his delivery. He was definitely not the same man she'd seen in that bar all those years ago. "It makes sense what he said about feeling his age and wanting to end on a high note, but to become a coach at a prep school? Back in Candlewood Falls? He swore to me he'd never return."

"We've all said never." Malbec arched his brow. "Both his sisters and his parents live here and he said he wanted to get back to what's important. Family."

"Right. He judged me so harshly for being loyal to mine."

Malbec chuckled. "Mom was manipulating you because she was scared you were going to run off and chase Dax from one hockey rink to the next. It's very different."

"I seriously can't believe he's actually moving back. And did you know he bought Barrelman's place?"

"I heard that from Dad this morning," Malbec said. "He said Dax is honoring the lease for the barn apartment."

"Lucky fucking me." The last thing she needed was her ex-boyfriend being her landlord.

"Eliza Jane and I are settled in our new place, and since Mom and Dad are shacking up again in the family home, Riesling and Trey moved into Dad's place, so there's the cottage on the winery and the cabin over at the doctor's office. I'm sure Riesling will let you stay there if you want."

"They've already rented it and Zinfandel is moving into the cottage. Mom already promised her. She wants to learn more about the business. She's real sharp with numbers. I can see her running that part it."

"So can I, but she's still too rough around the edges and needs to mature."

Chablis laughed. Their baby sister was like a wrecking ball. Much-needed, but always left a mess.

"I appreciate what you're doing, but I'm not going to let Dax run me out of my apartment. I've only been there a couple of months, but it's home to me. The barn has a separate driveway around the corner and is pretty far from the main house. I never saw the Barrelmans so I suspect I won't see Dax. Just so long as I don't see his flavor of the month coming and going, we'll be fine."

"He does like his arm candy."

She rolled her eyes. "Why am I'm letting him get under my skin? I'm so over him."

"Because you loved him with your entire soul and because you were pregnant and never told him. That's a lot to carry for seventeen years." Malbec lowered his chin. "Grandpa and Mom's secrets nearly destroyed us. This one is eating you from the inside out. This is the universe's way of telling you it's time to heal."

"I can't tell him what I did. If he doesn't hate me, he will now."

"Telling him wouldn't be about him. You'd be doing it for you. So you can heal and move on. Just like you've done with me and Mom. And that wasn't easy either."

"This is so different. This would hurt him to the core," she said. Her stomach rolled over. She and Dax had done and said some horrible things to each other, but not telling him was about the worst thing she could have done.

"It's slowly killing you." Malbec polished off his wine. "Do you want me to go see if he's gone?"

"No," she said softly. "Hiding from him like a child is stupid." She squared her shoulders and headed for the door. She swallowed her pulse. Time to face the past.

She stepped into the gift shop and her heart

dropped like a brick. Dax, all six foot three of him, stood by the small display Merlot had made in honor of the famous hockey star's return.

Merlot had created a special red blend called *Dax Fabion*. It would be a limited edition, only this year, and it went for two hundred dollars a bottle, with half the proceeds going to the children's hospital. They had paired it with some cheeses and candies, and Dax had graciously donated some signed items.

A group of local high school hockey players had come in with their coach to get a picture. Currently, Dax had his gaze focused on signing jerseys for the team.

He glanced up and winked at her.

It was hard not to smile.

"He looks good." Her mother looped her arm around her waist and gave it a little squeeze. "A few scars, some wrinkles, but still handsome."

Chablis wasn't going to argue the point, but she wasn't going to openly agree with her mom either.

"How did the team know he was going to be here?" Chablis turned to her mother.

"I asked him if he would stop by today."

"Of course you did."

Her mother had been talking about Dax for weeks. It's all she could think about. She'd become obsessed by it. Even more so than having two more grandchildren. Chablis found it to be odd and infuriating. Back when she'd been in high school, her mom used to tell her to forget about Dax because he was the kind of boy that was going to break her heart. Not because he was a bad person, but because he had a wandering soul. For their entire relationship, Chablis' parents did their best to make sure she understood that they did not believe Dax was marriage material. Not if he was going to continue chasing a pipe dream.

"We're raising money for sick kids," her mom said with a huff. "This isn't about you or the mistakes your father and I made when you were in high school or college."

"I'm glad we can agree you made mistakes."

"I thought we were past this. I know I said some horrible things to you in the past when Malbec left. I didn't mean them. I was trying to make Malbec change his mind."

"By destroying my confidence? By making me feel like you had no faith in me at all and then sticking with it?" Chablis wasn't angry with her mother, but it was so easy to take out her conflicting emotions about Dax on her mom.

"I was wrong in doing that. Telling you that I was scared and trying to protect my family isn't going to make you feel better."

"No. It's not," Chablis said, taking her mother's hand. She squeezed it. "I do understand, though."

"Sweetheart. I'm glad you're home. And I want you

to know that I'm so proud of what you've done with your life, but when are you going to give up being a firefighter and come work at the winery full-time where you belong?"

She jerked her hand away and let out a long breath. "Please don't push me. I'm in Candlewood Falls. I signed a year lease. I told you I'd give it a year. I won't go back on my word, but I need to have a safety net if things don't work out."

"You're thinking about running sooner," her mother said with more emotion than Chablis had heard in a while. "And that's because you still care for him."

"Let's not go there."

Her mom ran her hand up and down Chablis' back. Chablis considered taking a step back, but she decided that would only add to the tension. This really wasn't about her relationship with her mother, but about Dax.

"But him being home is affecting us," her mom said. "And don't say it's not. I can feel the tension growing. Don't pull away from me. Not now. Not over this. We've come too far."

Chablis leaned closer to her mom. She was right. "It's hard not to be catapulted back twenty years when I see him and that stirs the pot, which then makes me angry at you, Dad, and Malbec."

"I do understand. I'm here if you want to talk about it," her mom whispered. "But it looks like he's headed this way. I better go check inventory."

"Don't you dare leave me," Chablis said behind a clenched jaw.

But it fell on deaf ears.

She inhaled through her nose and blew it out slowly through her mouth while she tried not to stare at Dax as he strolled across the room with his killer smile.

"I was hoping I'd see you here." Gently, he touched her biceps and kissed her cheek.

God, he had such soft, full lips. She could remember how they felt on every inch of her body.

"Welcome back to Candlewood Falls." She took one small step back to keep from taking a huge sniff. He always smelled like he'd gone for a long stroll in a meadow filled with fresh pine. "I hear you're my new landlord."

"And I heard you're a firefighter as well as working at the winery."

"It's true. I couldn't give up my other career when I moved back to help out Malbec and Merlot."

"The three musketeers are back together and making wine," he said. "That's cool."

"It's nice to have us all in one place again." She laughed. "And getting along with my mom."

"She seems different."

"She's softer, but don't let that fool you. She's still the Weezer."

"I'll keep that in mind," he said with a chuckle. "Do you remember the morning I got caught sneaking out of your room? I thought your mother was going to chase me down the street with a shotgun."

"Malbec and my dad had to talk her out of it, though I'm sure the gun wouldn't have been loaded. She always did really like you."

"My dad used to tell me that if she didn't poison me that was a good sign," Dax said. "That and the fact she came to every single one of my home games."

"That she did." Her mother certainly gave mixed messages when it came to Dax except for one thing and that was she was not to leave town with him. She could be with him, even marry him, but only if he stayed in Candlewood Falls.

"Hey, listen," Dax said. "I was going to reach out if I didn't run into you today. I was hoping we could go out to dinner one night and catch up."

Her heart fluttered. She opened her mouth but wasn't sure how to respond. She cleared her throat. "I'm really busy between the fire department and here."

"You have to eat," he said. "Besides, I think we have some things to say to one another."

"It was a long time ago. There are no hard feelings."

He took her hand. "There are things I want to say. Please. Will you have dinner with me one night this week? And remember, I'm not past begging in very public ways."

She laughed, remembering him getting on his knees in the middle of her math class so she'd go on the haunted hayride with him. And that wasn't the only time he'd begged her to do something. If she didn't agree, he could be relentless. "What about tonight?" She didn't want to sit around and stew in her thoughts. She might as well get on with it.

"That's actually perfect. I'll pick you up at seven at your apartment?"

"Why don't I meet you at the diner in town? I can come straight from work."

"Nope." He shook his head. "I'm more in the mood for Gino's. I could go for some good pasta."

"Sounds good," she said.

"I'll see you there." He kissed her cheek and turned. He didn't make it out the door before a few other fans asked for autographs. He graciously gave them, along with posing for pictures. He glanced over his shoulder and waved as he headed out the door.

She sighed, giving her face a good fan. Out of the corner of her eye, she saw Zinfandel bouncing up and down as she raced across the room. That girl had way too much energy.

"He's so hot," Zinfandel said. "Tell me again why the two of you didn't work out?"

"I hope that's a rhetorical question." Chablis adored her baby sister, but sometimes she was a bit much to take.

"When I was driving into town, I saw Axel putting the finishing touches on his street art on the brewery. I bet it's going to be incredible. Axel is amazing."

"He sure is." Chablis rubbed her temples. "How

long do you think it will take for the good citizens of Candlewood Falls to get over Dax Fabion?"

"About the twelfth of never."

Dax

Dax pulled into his new home. As a kid he used to think if he could own a house like the Barrelman place, he'd arrived.

Now he could afford ten of them and still have money in the bank.

But none of that made him happy.

He'd done everything he'd set out to do when it came to his career. He'd even won the Stanley Cup.

Four times.

To everyone on the outside, his life was perfect. Except when he closed his eyes at night, all he could think about was Chablis and Candlewood Falls. The longer he stayed away, the more he missed both.

He tried pouring himself into being the best hockey player the sport had ever seen. For a while it worked.

Then he tried keeping the company of any woman who turned his head.

That never worked, but it did keep his mind occupied for a moment or two. But last year when Greg's wife was diagnosed with cancer and died a few months later, Dax realized that life was too short and he was barely living it. He needed to go home and try to make things right with the only woman he'd ever loved.

He pressed the garage door opener and eased his new SUV into its spot. Headlights flashed in his rearview mirror. He squinted, wondering who the hell was invading his personal space. Granted, the entire town knew the prodigal son had returned. They were having a big parade next weekend in his honor. He got that anytime he stepped foot in town people were going to stop him and ask for a picture or an autograph. He was used to that.

But he didn't want people stopping by his home.

"Hey, Dax. It's Axel."

"Oh. Hi." Except his friends would always get a pass and while he hadn't kept in touch with most people, he was looking forward to rekindling many friendships. "What brings you by?" He hadn't known Axel that well, but his brother Raf had been one of Dax's best friends growing up.

"I was on my home and saw you so I thought I'd give you an in-person invite." Axel stretched out his arm, which was covered in paint.

Dax shook his hand. "To what?"

"An unofficial unveiling of my masterpiece."

"I still can't believe the mayor had you do that." The only time Dax enjoyed being the center of attention was on the ice. He thrived on it then. Hearing the fans chant his name or the buzzer going off when he scored —it was intoxicating.

But outside of that, he hated it.

"Everyone is really excited to have you back and we'd like to do a little bachelor night over at the brewery Thursday night. Caleb, Malbec, Merlot, Raf, and Brad will be there."

"How can I turn down what's basically a high school reunion?" Dax laughed. "I look forward to it. Just text me the details."

"Will do," Axel said. "I'll let you get going. I'm sure you have a ton of unpacking to do."

"The truck was here all day and they did most of the heavy lifting. I just have to put shit away and I only have a couple of days to do it. Recruitment has started and there's a big tournament this weekend I have to spend time at, watching players and avoiding parents." That was a sentence he never thought he'd say. Of all the things he thought he'd be doing after retirement, coaching a high school prep team wasn't one of them.

College, maybe. And he did have his name in the hat with three different division one schools.

But if he was being honest with himself, when he left Candlewood Falls at the ripe old age of seventeen, he figured when he retired he'd go into sportscasting. But when he left, he thought Chablis was going to come with him.

"They are lucky to have you and this town is happy you're back." Axel smiled. "See you Thursday."

Dax waited for Axel to pull out of the driveway

before closing the garage and heading into his new digs.

The house was a seven-thousand-square-foot two-story dwelling. It had been remodeled about four years ago in a farmhouse style and Dax loved it so much that he talked Barrelman into selling most of the furniture. He strolled across the back entryway, through the living room and into the bar area. He poured himself a scotch on the rocks and stared out the picture window at the barn turned into an apartment.

His cell buzzed in his back pocket. He pulled it out and glanced at the text on the screen from one of his sisters.

Camila: *I'm about to drive by your place. Nova is with me. Mind if we stop by?*

Dax: *Come on over.*

He'd had lunch with his parents, but had yet to see either of his sisters since rolling into town. While they both worked in the school system, one as a teacher and one as a social worker, they both also coached sports, so they were always busy after the school day ended.

Dax tapped the home icon on his phone and turned on the front lights and made sure the door was unlocked.

Dax: *Door's open. Just come in. I'll open a bottle of red.*

Both his sisters loved wine. A lot. And he'd already made sure he stocked their favorites. He planned on having them over for dinner at least once a week, if not more, for as long as he lived here.

Based on the way Chablis received him, he had his work cut out in winning her back. But he suspected that would be the case. However, he was confident there was still something there, which was why he bought this house and why he took the job with the Candlewood Falls Prep School.

But still, he had to be realistic and he needed a backup plan.

After opening a bottle of wine so it could breathe, he moved a couple of boxes out of the room.

"Lucy, I'm home," his sister Nova called.

"You've got some explaining to do," he said with a chuckle. When they were kids, they used to love to watch old reruns of the *I Love Lucy* show and they almost always greeted each other in this manner.

"You two are so weird." Camila wrapped her arms around him and gave him a big hug. "To this day, I don't understand your obsession with that show."

"It's so freaking funny." Dax embraced his other sister. It felt so good to be this close to his family again. As much as he'd loved his career, he'd missed his siblings. "It's one of the best sitcoms ever made and Lucile Ball is the funniest woman that ever lived."

"No. Betty White was." Camila took the glass of wine he offered and plopped down on his plush leather sofa. "My God. This is amazing."

"I still can't believe you bought this house." Nova kicked off her shoes and snuggled in next to her sister, sipping her wine. "After you closed, I got the keys from

Mom and Dad and I snuck in a couple of times, giving myself the tour. Can I come over and take a soak in your tub?"

"Anytime you want." He topped off his scotch and made himself comfortable in the recliner.

"So, you know we never pull any punches," Nova said. "Have you seen Chablis yet?"

He should have known that his sisters didn't come over *just* to shoot the shit, especially when it was after eight in the evening. Of course they had an agenda. "I ran into her when I stopped by the winery for a brief public appearance that her mom set up."

"How is she?"

"Weezer's the same old Weezer," he said.

"Come on." Nova uncrossed her legs. "You know that's not who we're asking about."

"Seriously? You're going to ask me that when neither one of you left this town except for college and you see her all the time? You probably had lunch with her last week."

"You know that's not true," Camila said. "Chablis moved away the same time Malbec did and she didn't come around for years. She barely spoke to anyone in her family, and she's only been back for a few months. She works two jobs and when we've asked her to join us for a cocktail or something, she always turns us down, with the exception of once and that was before you took the job at CWF Prep."

"She's busy," Dax said. He understood why Chablis

might not want to get together with his family. He might make up excuses if anyone other than Malbec or maybe Merlot asked him out for a beer. He didn't know her younger siblings that well. They were toddlers when he was in high school, and Riesling was closer to Nova's age. Not to mention when she'd been a kid, she chased everyone around with a stethoscope, wanting to play doctor. She was almost as scary as her mother. "Besides, when I was at the winery, two people made dumb-ass comments about her and me and the good old days. I'm sure she doesn't want to hear that any more than I do."

"Are you trying to tell us that you don't still have feelings for her?" Camila asked.

Headlights appeared in the picture window. The car slowed as it crossed in front of the house. A red flashing light from the blinker lit up the night sky. The vehicle turned into the driveway to the barn.

Chablis was home.

His pulse picked up a notch. He avoided the urge to stand up and race across the room to check out if indeed the car drove down the long driveway or if it was just making the turn down Potter Place. "She was my first love; I'll always care about her." If he wasn't partially honest with his sisters, they'd never leave it alone.

"She's your *only* love," Nova said under her breath. "Every other woman you've dated was a bimbo."

"Don't insult my dating life or the ladies I've been

with." While he couldn't deny that he'd never loved anyone other than Chablis, he didn't like his sisters putting down anyone. It wasn't a good look. "I might not have the best luck, but some of my past girlfriends were really sweet."

"Not a single one of them were marriage material," Camila said.

"I'm not interested in settling down." He nearly choked on his lie. But there was only one person he wanted to spend the rest of his life with, and if he couldn't have her, he'd rather be alone. Why try to work on being happy with someone that couldn't bring him the kind of joy that only Chablis could? Besides, that would only make two people incredibly miserable.

"You wanted to marry Chablis," Nova said with that singsong voice of hers.

"I wanted her to give up her dreams for mine. That had misery and divorce written all over it." He took a gulp of his scotch. "I'd like the two of you to drop this. What Chablis and I had ended when she chose to stick with her mom's plan, which for the—"

"But she didn't," Nova said. "After she graduated, she ran off and became a firefighter."

"I know that. She came and told me what happened." He'd never told his family about her visit. Or that he'd walked away. For an entire year he thought about racing home and begging for her forgiveness, but then he'd remember how she'd ripped it apart the day she'd packed her bags and said she was coming with him, but didn't follow through.

And then again at her graduation.

She couldn't break ties with her family until Malbec did it for her. What would have happened if Malbec had come back? She would have too and where would that have left them?

But it wasn't just her. It was him too. He had to come to the realization that he wanted his career more than he wanted her and that was a hard pill to swallow. He'd been selfish. He had expected her to follow him like a little groupie. As if his life was more important than hers and that had been the most unfair thing he'd ever asked her to do and he hated himself for it. The sad part about all of it was that he'd truly loved her; he was just young and immature, and as humble as he'd been about his talent, he hadn't been that way about the love they shared. He took her problems with her family as an assault on their relationship.

"You knew she left Candlewood Falls and her family business and you didn't fight for her?" Camila leaned forward and glared. "What the hell is wrong with you?"

"A lot," he admitted, but he wasn't about to give that laundry list to his siblings. "Look. I need you to stay out of my personal business with Chablis. We hurt each pretty badly and I'd like to make amends with her." He held up his hand. "That doesn't mean I want to get back together with her. All it means is that I want her and I to be in a good place."

"Sounds like you're full of shit and only spewing this crap in case she rejects you."

Jesus, his sisters were smart.

"You can think whatever helps you sleep at night, but it's not true." He could only hope he was as good at covering up his true feelings as his sisters were intuitive. "I love you both, but please don't play matchmaker."

"You can relax; we wouldn't dare." Camila raised her glass. "But one of the reasons we wanted to stop by was that we overheard Mom speaking with Weezer today."

Dax's heart dropped like a ton of bricks to his gut. "Good Lord. Why? They were never all that close." His mom had been head of the PTA at the public school where both his sisters went and all the River kids went. Dax started there, but by the time he hit middle school, it was obvious to everyone that he had a gift and in ninth grade he went to Candlewood Falls Prep, where his mother also volunteered.

Weezer called her the queen of helicopter parenting.

Which wasn't true.

Dorothy Fabion let her kids fall flat on their faces, and they all did, more than once. But because they had the kind of privilege that allowed her to stay at home with her kids, she could be more involved than most.

Dax had to admit that sometimes it was too much, but it wasn't just him and his sisters that benefited from her hard work. It was the entire school ecosystem.

She worked hard for all the kids. And she continued to do so now as she sat on the board.

"What the hell were they talking about?" Dax set his drink on the end table and leaned forward.

"They're meeting for coffee at the Green Bean at eight," Nova said.

"That's interesting." Dax rose and strolled to the picture window. He stuffed his hands in his pockets and stared out the window. The car had disappeared, but the lights were on in the barn apartment. They hadn't been on before. "What else did you hear?"

"For someone who isn't interested in Chablis, you're certainly quite concerned about what Mom and Weezer are going to say to each other," Camila said.

"One has nothing to do with the other." He took in a slow breath. The last thing he needed was Weezer and his mother meddling. That had disaster written all over it. But he wouldn't put it past either one of them.

In his youth, Weezer did her best to remind Dax that his career, if he chose to pursue it, would take him from one city to the next, and possibly not bring in a lot of money. That he was talented in their small town. That he might be great in prep school or even juniors, but that he'd be just another hockey player when he got to the big leagues.

As for his mother, well, she would tell him that she worried about him not branching out and dating other girls. That neither one of them could really experience love until they had lived a little. But the real kicker had been when she told him that he was stealing her dreams when he asked her to take this leap with him. It wouldn't surprise him if his mom had put little bugs in Chablis' ear either.

"I'll talk to Mom in the morning," he said. "Thanks for letting me know."

"We're both glad you're back." Nova eased behind him and squeezed his shoulder.

He wrapped his arm around his little sister. "I am too." This was where he belonged. Now he just needed Chablis to open her arms and welcome him home too.

2

WEEZER

Weezer snagged her iced coffee and bagel off the counter at the Green Bean. She glanced over her shoulder, making note of everyone. It would be considered normal for her to be in the establishment at any given time during the day, any day of the week.

Only, it could be considered out of the ordinary for her to be meeting Dorothy Fabion for breakfast.

Weezer scurried to the outside patio. She scanned the area and couldn't find the woman who had texted her five minutes ago informing her she'd already gotten a table. She pulled out her cell and read the message again.

Dorothy: *Here. Back table by the trees.*

Weezer glanced up and looked around again. That's when she spotted Dorothy way in the back. Practically in the bushes. Weezer wasn't sure if that was a good thing or a bad thing. She made her way across the patio. "Good morning," she said.

"Weezer." Dorothy nodded. "I have to tell you that my husband and I cracked the new blend in my son's name and it's delicious."

"I'm glad you liked it, but I hope you're saving a few bottles. It's a limited collection." Weezer sat down and opened up her everything bagel with cream cheese. "I also hope that whoever sold it to you gave you a few bottles on the house."

"Oh. They did and it wasn't necessary."

"It absolutely was. Your son was one of the best hockey players the sport has ever seen and I'm thrilled that we had the privilege to honor him that way." Weezer also had so much to make up for, but she couldn't get into all the details of that with Dorothy. This meeting was about how they were going to help their children mend the fences that they helped tear apart. "He stopped by yesterday and he's as handsome and sweet as ever. He stayed longer than I had asked and took pictures and signed autographs and didn't complain once. I know he must hate that part of his career."

"It's not his favorite, that's for sure," Dorothy said. "But he understands it's the part that means the most. Without the fans, it was all for nothing." Dorothy fiddled with her coffee and lowered her gaze. "What we did when our kids were in high school might have helped their careers, but I'm not sure it helped in their happiness."

"Probably not," Weezer said.

"I can't believe I went to his team captain and asked him to help Dax get over Chablis."

"I can." Weezer arched a brow. "No offense, Dorothy. But you were always a bit of a helicopter parent."

"No, I wasn't, and I resent you calling me that."

Weezer jerked her head back.

"Oh, don't act as if you're offended. Let's not pretend anymore." Dorothy smirked, but it wasn't a condescending one. It was more playful. "I didn't believe as strongly as you did that they weren't meant for each other, but once he was drafted, I didn't want his hard work to be split in two. But the timing of Malbec leaving and her showing up couldn't have been more cruel for either one of them. I still lose sleep over that one."

"Truth be told, so do I." Weezer took a long sip of her cold, bitter drink. "But I also can't believe it worked. It makes me wonder if Dax really loved her as much as he said he did."

"Oh, they loved each other. Still do," Dorothy said. "Five years ago, whenever anyone asked Dax what he would do if he retired, coaching at a prep school never came out of his mouth. Maybe a division one college or professional, but he usually mentioned broadcasting, if he answered the question. So, he came back because of Chablis."

"When he made the decision, Chablis wasn't living in Candlewood Falls. She was three towns over."

"Which isn't that far away," Dorothy said. "I know my son. Twenty years ago he was singularly focused. Make the NHL. Chablis was supposed to be part of that; however, he didn't believe he was anything without hockey. That was our fault."

"I pushed all my older kids right out the door. I wasn't about to make the same mistake with the twins and Zinfandel. I let them choose. They stayed in the wine business, but they didn't choose to work for me." Weezer held up her finger. "Yet. But they all stayed in Candlewood Falls."

"I'm not sure we made a mistake all those years ago. Maybe they needed to live a little. Make their own way. Do their own thing."

"You know they won't see it that way if they knew about all the things we did. All the schemes we came up with between your extra hockey lessons and hockey camps and my crazy rules to keep those two from spending too much time together, right down to telling her she couldn't do it without Malbec, knowing he was going to take off."

"I'm sorry. I know that was hard for you."

Weezer nodded. "One of the hardest things I've ever done. And I'm sorry it put you in the position it did with going to Greg, Dax's team captain."

Dorothy reached across the table and took Weezer's hand. "We did what we thought was best for our children and I was happy to help you. We both know what could have happened if Chablis moved to Buffalo. No one can fault us for wanting to do the right thing for our families."

Weezer laughed. "Our kids sure can."

"Oh. Don't I know it. Did you know he dated that older hussy for like three months? I cringed having to have dinner with her. When I asked Greg to set him up, I thought he understood I wanted it to be a nice girl. After that, all he brought home were girls that could only be considered flavors of the month."

"Honey. That's only because he couldn't get Chablis out of his mind. Now they are both back, and hello, living right next door to each other. That should make it easier for them to find each other."

"Maybe we should stay out of it," Dorothy said.

"Are you serious?"

Dorothy smiled. "About as serious as you would be if you said it." Her smile turned into a frown. "Oh shit. Don't turn around."

"What? Why?"

"My son is here."

Dax

Dax leaned against the tree where his mom or Weezer couldn't see him for about ten minutes. Sadly, he couldn't hear them and he wasn't good at reading lips either.

But what he did get from watching them was they were better friends than anyone suspected.

Or knew.

Of course, that was true of Weezer and most people in town.

Anyone who was close to her almost always pretended they weren't. Not because they were embarrassed or ashamed or afraid of what anyone would think. It certainly wasn't because they were scared of Weezer either. But anyone who was a true friend to Weezer valued that friendship.

Interesting that his mother might be in that inner circle.

He had to wonder if that happened before his career with the NHL started.

Or after.

He glanced at his watch. He was meeting Brad Wilde for breakfast and then off to the ice rink. Time to make his presence known.

He meandered around a couple tables and made eye contact with his mother. He smiled.

She did not.

"Good morning, Mother," he said, mildly amused. "Weezer. Fancy seeing the two of you here."

"It's the best coffee in town." Weezer raised her

mug. "And ever since my husband moved back into the house, he's trying to regulate how much of this I drink. He thinks too much caffeine makes me ornery when that's my natural state."

Dax laughed. Weezer's bark was worse than her bite, but it had taken him years to figure that out. "I promise not to tell Carter."

"I thought you had appointments at the rink all day," his mom said.

"I do, but I'm heading over to Brad's this morning. I haven't seen him in years. Why didn't you tell me he has a daughter?" He pulled up a chair. "And he's living with Lyra Chambers? Holy hell. That's an interesting pairing. I didn't go to the same high school as everyone else in this town, but I sure as hell remember what a snob she was."

"For the most part, she's changed," Weezer said. "But her mother hasn't."

"That's for darn sure." His mother nodded. "Lyra and Brad balance each other and their kids sure are sweet."

Weezer stood. "I really need to get back to the winery. It was good to catch up with you, Dorothy. Talk soon." Weezer squeezed Dax's shoulder. "Don't be a stranger. You know you're welcome in my home anytime. As a matter of fact, why don't you come over for Sunday supper. It will be like old times. Everyone will be there."

"I'd like that," Dax said. "Thank you for the invite."

"Dinner is at six, as usual, but feel free to come over any time after three. We'll be having games in the yard and Ashling is playing a one-person play. That's always entertaining." Weezer smiled. "Enjoy the day." She turned and moved like a cat, slinking her way through the maze of tables.

Dax leaned back. "So, you and the Weezer, eh?"

"Just because you spent some time in Canada playing juniors doesn't make you Canadian," his mother said with a fair amount of sarcasm.

"I was just a little surprised to see you and Weezer sitting together. It's not like the two of you are best friends."

"We're not enemies," his mother said. "She's the most misunderstood woman in this town and ever since Malbec returned, she's been a much softer version of her old self and I like her." His mother folded her arms across her chest like a defiant child.

He nearly burst out laughing. "I'm glad about that, but I don't trust that the two of you aren't scheming on ways to get Chablis and me together. I won't have that, Mother."

"Don't call me that. I hate it."

"I know. That's why I pick the perfect times to do it." He leaned forward and took her hands. He kept his focus on her eyes, never letting his gaze waver. Most kids were afraid of Weezer, not his mom. He, on the other hand, would have rather been disciplined by Chablis' mom than deal with the look of disappointment that he'd put on his mom's face a time or two. His heart fluttered. He never liked hurting his mom's feelings, but sometimes it was a necessary evil. "I'm only going to say this once. Don't play matchmaker with me and Chablis."

"I'm not."

"No offense, but I don't believe you." He lowered his chin. "For the record, I've asked Chablis to have dinner with me tonight."

"That sounds like a date."

He inhaled sharply and blew it out in a huff. "No. It's not. It's two people who have a world of hurt between them making amends. Nothing more, nothing less. I told my sisters last night, Dad before I got here, and now I'm telling you. Chablis and I were high school sweethearts. Our romance ran its course. All I want is for the two of us to be able to pass each other in the street and not feel uncomfortable around each other."

She squeezed. "You feel bad around Chablis?"

Boy, was that a loaded question. "Yes. I do. I hurt her and I owe her an apology."

"She hurt you too."

He nodded. He wouldn't argue that point. But he wasn't going to dwell on the past. It was time to move into the future. "That was a long time ago. I want her to know that I'm going to be a good landlord and there's no reason for her to move."

"Does she want to?"

"She's made mention of it to the estate when I bought the house, but so far, she hasn't asked to be let out of her lease. I want to assure her she can have the barn apartment as long as she wants. And at the price she's paying. Hell, if I didn't think she'd get so damn insulted, I'd let her live there for free."

"I'm glad to hear that, but she's too proud, like her mother."

He chuckled. "Just promise me that whatever you and Weezer have cooking, you'll put the brakes on."

"We haven't planned anything. Swear to God." His mother crossed her fingers, holding them up. "However, you're fooling yourself if you think you're over that young woman, and I know this because you're going out of your way to make sure we all know that you are."

That was all true, but he was sticking to his guns because if both families didn't back off, he didn't stand a chance.

He stood and kissed his mother's cheek. "If that's true, all the more reason for you to stay out of it." He didn't give his mother a chance to retort. He stuffed his hands in his pockets and made a beeline for the front door. He had twenty minutes to make it across town to his buddy Brad's house and breakfast with him and his family.

Family.

Perhaps someday that would be him.

For now, he'd settle for tonight's dinner.

3

CHABLIS

Chablis groaned as she followed Serena to the outdoor seating area with her heart in her throat. All day she could barely concentrate on her work at the winery. Her mind kept wandering back to Dax. It didn't help that she sat outside with her morning tea and watched him sip his juice, shirtless, while he stared out at the rising sun on his back deck.

Old man Barrelman never did that.

Thank God.

Of course, now all she could think about was Dax's bare chest.

"So, you're meeting Dax. I find that interesting after all these years. Are the two of you starting things up again?" Serena asked.

"We're old friends having dinner." Chablis knew Serena's son had applied to CFW Prep and was looking to make the hockey team. But the history between her

60

husband and Dax was strained, at least on Toby's part. Dax always tried to keep his cool where Toby was concerned.

"I wonder what happened to make him retire so abruptly. And to take a job as a coach to high school boys. I mean, there has to be a story there."

"No story. It was just time and his family is here." Chablis gritted her teeth. She shouldn't be talking for Dax, but Serena always had a way of getting under her skin. "Are you going to be our waitress? Because if you are, could I get a scotch on the rocks?"

"You know I only work here part-time to get out of the house. We don't need the money." Serena planted a hand on her hip. "Are you sure you wouldn't rather a glass of wine? We do have a fine selection of your family's wine to choose from."

"Scotch. Please."

"Would you like the reserve?"

"No. The house brand is fine."

"I'll be right back with that." Serena stuck her nose in the air and took off toward the bar.

One of the hardest things about being a River was being expected to like the finer brands of alcohol. Sometimes it just wasn't that important. She blew out a puff of air and glanced toward the sky. The stars were out in spades. She was glad Dax had been able to get a reservation on the patio on such short notice. But it wasn't the weekend.

She pulled her wrap around her as one of the busboys came around and adjusted the heater.

It also wasn't overly hot either.

"Sorry I'm late." A familiar voice echoed in the night air like warm fudge covering cold ice cream.

She smiled. "I've only been here about five minutes."

He leaned in and kissed her cheek.

Part of her wanted to turn her face and find his lips for old times' sake.

A few people in the restaurant waved or pointed. Others whispered.

He smiled and waved in return.

"Doesn't that make you crazy?" she asked.

"Honestly, yes. But not in my hometown. Half these people I remember from when I was a boy."

Serena reappeared with Chablis' drink. "Well, hello, Dax." She did a little dance, shifting her weight back and forth. "Twice in the same day. It must be fate. I must say, my son usually plays so much better, but we're struggling with a new parent coach. You know how that goes." She shook her head. "Toby normally coaches but the board thought he'd been coaching the same group too long. They told him he could pick another level or take a break. Hockey politics. Ridiculous." She rolled her eyes. "Anyway. I'm sure TJ will do so much better tomorrow."

"Like I said in the stands, I won't be talking with

any of the parents about their kids. That includes you, Serena."

"It's kind of hard not to talk to me right now since I'll be taking your order. Speaking of which, what can I get you to drink? It's on the house. It's the least I can do for our hometown hero."

"No. It's not. I cannot accept that. And you shouldn't offer," Dax said firmly. "Someone might think you're bribing the coach."

"That's the silliest thing I've ever heard." Serena folded her hands over her chest. "And I'm not offering. The restaurant is. I can't believe you'd accuse me of something like that. You should know me better than that. Besides, you can talk to management if you'd like."

"That may be the case, but I think it's best if I pay for my drink, thank you."

She dropped her hands to her sides. "Fine. What would you like?"

"I'll take a scotch," Dax said. "Make it a double. Thank you."

Chablis lifted her glass and gulped. "I still can't stand her," she said after Serena was out of earshot.

"She's a nightmare in the stands and Toby is way too hard on his kid." Dax laughed. "He's living through his son, who isn't very disciplined. He's arrogant and doesn't take direction well. He's been told his entire life he's better than everyone else when he's not. Well, he's good.

Better than most. But he gets in his own way. Now, he's playing in a tournament where he's not shining, and his parents are blaming it on poor coaching. Toby actually cornered me today and told me that the reason his kid didn't have a stellar performance was because he's struggling with this new coach and the way he runs the bench, but that he was proud that his son didn't lose his cool on the ice. But the reality is that his boy made selfish choices, and there is nothing wrong with his coach."

"Better be quiet; here she comes."

Playfully, Dax rolled his eyes, mimicking Serena.

Serena set the drink down and quickly left.

"Toby desperately wants his kid to do what he couldn't, and Serena is just as batty as ever. She still doesn't understand the game." Dax chugged half of his drink. "I remember my first travel coach telling us that he'd been coaching youth sports for ten years and that he'd never had a kid go to the NHL and he suspected that maybe he'd be lucky if he had one."

"How many did he end up coaching that played professional hockey?"

"You're looking at the one." Dax rubbed the back of his neck. "I'm sorry. It has been one hell of a long day. Toby wasn't the worst of the parents in the stands. Actually, all he does is coach his boy, which is hard because TJ listens to him and not his coach. But Serena is horrible. She's screaming at everyone. And both of them are going to make it hard for me. If I cut their kid, they are going to think it's going to be all about the fact that Toby and I never liked each other."

"No. Toby was jealous of you, and Serena never liked me much because her mother didn't like mine."

"Weezer is the most misunderstood woman in this town. But that's changing."

Chablis nodded. Her mom had made a lot of changes, but she did enjoy keeping a lot of people in Candlewood Falls at arm's length. "What are you going to do about them?"

"I'm going to be fair. That's all I can do," he said. "My folks warned me how horrible parents of hockey players can be."

"I remember that one playoff game I went to your first year at CFW Prep. Malbec, Brad, and Caleb all came with me, but they sat in the pit with all the other kids. I sat with your parents. There was one dad who screamed horrible things every single time your feet hit the ice. He was not happy that you had made the team."

"There were a few of those on every team I was on. But fortunately for me it was because I was good, not because I was an asshole. But enough shop talk. How was your day?"

"Uneventful," she said. "It usually is at the winery. It's nice when it's that way at the station."

"I can't believe you became a firefighter." Dax shook his head. "Of all the things I could imagine you doing, that wasn't one of them. How did you decide to do that?"

"Long story short, I put a bunch of career choices in a hat and that was one of them."

"I have to ask. What were the others?"

"A cop. A teacher. A singer. A—"

"You only sang for me," he said with an arched brow. "You swore to me you'd never sing for the masses."

She lifted her scotch and took a slow draw. Singing wasn't something she liked to do in public. She reserved it for the privacy of her shower. "I'm glad I didn't pick that one," she said. "Or one that required me to carry a gun. I'm a horrible shot."

"You've been shooting?"

"I dated a guy who belonged to a gun club," she admitted. Not that she wanted to talk about past boyfriends, but he asked, so what the hell. Also, it showed she didn't sit around pining after him all these years. "It became our Friday night date thing. I actually kind of hated it."

"I haven't shot a rifle since Malbec and Caleb took me out in the back of the winery. I was scared shitless your mom was going to catch us and chase us through the center of town."

"If you all thought she didn't know, then you all were stupid as shit." Chablis' heartbeat had yet to settle. He had the same effect on her as he always had and she wished she resented it, but instead she enjoyed the way it made her feel alive, which she hadn't felt in a long time.

It was as if he ignited a fire inside her that had been smoldering since she left him in Buffalo seventeen years ago.

"I mean, it was a twenty-two rifle. It makes a loud noise when you fire it. Besides, Malbec had permission. He was just messing with you."

"Are you serious?"

Chablis smiled. "Behind the trees was a barrier so the bullets didn't travel too far in case you missed the target. Mom didn't want you hitting anyone or anything. But she wanted you boys to have a little fun without going out and doing something really stupid. She called your parents and everything."

"You learn something new every day." He raised his glass and clanked it against hers.

She took a small sip. The last thing she wanted to do was get drunk. Feeling relaxed was one thing, but even buzzed would be too much. She needed to keep her head on straight or she'd end up begging him to take her to bed. She was notorious for doing that, and then she'd wake up telling him it was a mistake. That his world wasn't her world and it would never work.

When her mother had crushed her confidence and she found herself pregnant, she went to Dax believing they could just pick up where they'd left off, only they'd never had the relationship that other teenagers or young adults had.

Dax wasn't a normal kid. He was a superstar. He was going zero to sixty in two seconds and nothing was going to stop him.

Nothing.

When his parents moved him into the dorms at CWF Prep his sophomore year, that was the beginning of his transformation to being a machine. He spent two years in that school and while she got to see him on a regular basis, he wasn't his own person.

He was a hockey player with a one-way ticket to the NHL. Everything he did was in an effort to obtain a singular goal. When he left for juniors in Canada, she knew deep down that their plans for her to follow him after she graduated from high school was just talk.

Their love was real, but the rest was a fantasy. There was no way they could have it all. For Dax, it was either he chased his dream, leaving her behind, or he didn't.

And he never really gave her a second thought.

"Earth to Chablis." Dax waved his drink under her nose. "Where'd you go?"

"I was just thinking about the past."

"I've been doing that a lot lately. It's hard not to since the second I stepped back in this town," he said. "I hope it's good memories."

"Good and bad." She folded her hands, rested them in her lap, and picked at her thumbnail.

"Do you care to share?" He leaned forward, tilting his head.

"It's a hodgepodge of things." She blew out a puff of

air as Serena approached. She would continue to put a damper on the evening. All through high school, Serena made things a competition between them. It was bad enough that half the time their boyfriends were on opposing travel teams before they both made the CFW Prep team.

But that's where things got even worse. Because Dax was the star, and Toby was always in his shadow, it added a lot of tension on and off the ice. They weren't friends, and Chablis didn't care for Serena, but because of the team, they were constantly doing things together. But at every turn, Serena tried to make Dax or Chablis look bad. It was never too horrible. She wasn't that kind of a mean girl, but she wasn't nice either.

"Are you ready to order?" Serena asked with a bright smile.

"Yes," she said. "First, I'll take a glass of the River Winery Cabernet, and then I'll have your pasta special."

"I'll have the same," Dax said.

"Good choice," Serena said. "I'll put that order in right away. And I do have to say we are happy to welcome you back to Candlewood Falls and to CFW Prep. You're going to make for a great coach." She turned on her heel and took off.

"Unbelievable," Dax muttered.

"She's special." Chablis polished off her scotch, getting the courage she needed. "You mentioned yesterday there were things you wanted to discuss with me, which is why we're having dinner together."

He leaned back and lifted his arm, resting it on the back of his chair. "I was hoping to get to that later in the evening."

"I've got a twenty-four shift tomorrow at the station. As soon as dinner is over, I need to get home and get some sleep. Work starts at seven and I have a forty-minute commute."

"I can respect that," he said. "Now that I'm sitting here, I'm not sure where to begin." He glanced toward the sky.

Serena brought them their wine; thankfully she kept her mouth closed this time. This gave him a few minutes to figure out whatever it was that had been rattling around in his brain.

Even as a teenager, he'd been contemplative. Always choosing his words carefully, unless he'd been pissed off. Then watch out because he had a razor-sharp tongue.

She couldn't decide if this was good or bad.

"Do you remember my first NHL game?" he asked.

She flattened her hand against her stomach. "Yes. You were amazing." She didn't want to talk about what had transpired after the game, so she focused on his accomplishments. "To hear the crowd welcome you like —wow—my heart was in my throat I was so excited for you. That had been everything you had worked so hard for your entire life."

"Thanks," he said. "My first shift. When my feet hit the ice, I glanced up to the area of the arena that you used to sit in whenever you'd come to my games. I knew it was silly because first, no way could I see you in a crowd like that and second, why would you come to that game. You told me we were done. That being with me again was a mistake. For both of us and that I should forget you and move on."

"I am my mother's daughter," she said softly. To hear her words so harshly vocalized back at her made her stomach churn. "I'm sorry about the things I said. I did it only to hurt you so you'd go back to Buffalo and let me go."

"Deep down, I knew that." He nodded. "It wasn't the first time you'd done that to me." He lowered his chin. "Two years before that you showed up in Canada with a suitcase and declared you were dropping out of college."

She groaned. "If I had known this was going to be a reminder of how cruel I could be, I would have gone home and eaten leftovers."

"No. That's not what I want this to be," he said. "When I left your graduation, I swore that was it. I would never let you back in and that I would do whatever it took to get over you."

"I'd say you did a good job of that and pretty quickly."

He chuckled. "If you're talking about Traci, I'd only met her that night."

Chablis' heart sank. "Are you serious?"

"Yes. My captain fixed me up with her and we did

end up dating for a few months. She was the start of my fascination with older women for a while."

"I did notice that in the newspaper," Chablis admitted. "For the record, my family was always obsessed with your hockey career."

The corner of his mouth lifted into a half smile. "What about you?"

"You know I love hockey." She shrugged. "I can't believe you pretended she was your girlfriend." Bile rose to her throat. "I really believed you cared about her."

"I did. Just not that night."

"I'm sorry, but that's not making me feel better." She sucked in a deep breath and let it come out her nose like an angry bull. "I came there to tell you how I felt about you." And that she was pregnant, but for now she'd continue to keep that to herself. A restaurant wasn't the place to break that news to him. She'd do that in private, and not when she was angry. That wouldn't be good. "And you purposely hurt me."

"I did it to protect myself," he said. "Because I was afraid if I let you in, you'd do the same thing you've always done. Leave me in the morning."

She opened her mouth, but slammed it shut. He had a point. Only, she wouldn't have done that, but he couldn't have known because she hadn't told him the truth. "There are things that you don't know. That I didn't tell you," she whispered. Her eyes burned.

"What do you mean?" He reached across the table and took her hand. "You look upset."

She fought the tears with everything she had. She would not cry in front of him. Not tonight. Not in this restaurant. "When I came to you that night I was broken. My mother had told me I wasn't good enough."

"You know that's not true."

"But I didn't." She wished she could nod her head in agreement; however, even today she wasn't sure. "I had just graduated with the degree my mother told me to get so I could do what my mother and father expected me to do. I had told you, the man I loved, that I didn't really love you all that much. All I knew was that my life was literally upside down and I didn't know what to do."

"So you came running to me."

"You make that sound as if it's a bad thing."

"I'm sorry. I didn't realize this would bring up all these old emotions to the surface." He reached across the table and took her hand again. "This might sting," he said softly. "I told myself after you left the bar that if you were still there in the morning, you might be willing to fight for us. But when I went looking for you the next day, you'd hightailed it home."

"You made yourself clear."

"Sounds like we had a lot of communication problems when we were kids." He squeezed before releasing her hand and leaning backward. "I asked you to dinner because I wanted to apologize for hurting you. For playing games with your emotions. But also because I believe I was sabotaging us from the beginning."

She blinked. Her therapist had told her for years that she'd been doing that all along. And she knew that to be true.

But she struggled to believe that was something Dax participated in.

"My coaches. My trainers. Even my parents all told me that if I wanted to go all the way, I couldn't have any distractions and you were exactly that. I pretended to ignore them. I told myself that I could have you and my career, but I kept you at arm's length. I never fully let you in and for that I'm deeply sorry."

"Wow." She had to admit, even if to herself, that she often wondered if accepting her place as second fiddle to hockey in Dax's life would end up destroying them had she followed him to Buffalo, which is one of the reasons she never did.

Of course, she hadn't come to that realization until she'd been in therapy.

"That's deep," she said.

"It's true."

"I suppose we both did a little bit of that. I mean, people had a lot of expectations for you and my family had theirs for me and neither one of us wanted to disappoint them."

"I have to be honest with you," he said. "I wanted to be a pro hockey player so badly and as much as I loved you and wanted you in my life, I was willing to screw it up to have my career, even though I said I wasn't."

She felt her eyes go wide and her jaw drop open. That was the last thing she ever thought she'd hear Dax Fabion say to her. "So, what you're saying is that even if I wasn't a yo-yo ride, we wouldn't have made it? You would have found a way to break us up." Maybe she didn't need to tell him her dark secret. Maybe she didn't need to hurt him anymore. Had he never come back to town, she'd never even think of telling him anyway.

Though, that wasn't entirely true. She thought about that all the time.

"You kicking me to the curb over and over again made it easy for me to concentrate on my training. I focused all my hurt, anger, and frustration into that. When I finally made it and I had my first taste of what it was going to be like out there, it was bittersweet. I wanted you with me. For the first two years I thought maybe I'd made a mistake by sending you away that night, but I couldn't bring myself to call you. The longer I waited, the more things changed. I heard about your life through my parents. I heard about your engagement and that's when—"

"You know I was engaged?"

He nodded. "I didn't find out you never got married until about a year ago."

"Well, that relationship only lasted two years and

the engagement three months. It was doomed from the beginning."

"Why?" Dax asked. "If you don't mind me asking."

"I was working on my relationship with Malbec and my mom, and he didn't think I should. He thought my mom was crass and overbearing and thought it would be better if I completely cut her out of my life."

"Oh. He never got to know your family too well because that was never happening. Even I knew better than to ask that of you."

"He also thought me being a firefighter was something I should give up once we got married and had kids," she said. "He had it in his head that I was going to stay at home or something."

"I couldn't see you doing that," he said. "Here comes Serena with our dinner. How much do you want to bet that she brings up hockey or her kid again?"

"I'm not taking that bet."

"Here you go." Serena placed the food on the table. "Toby called while I was in the kitchen. I told him that you were here and he wanted me to extend an invite to our house for dinner one night this week."

Chablis felt the corners of her mouth twitch.

"Thanks, but I can't. Not until after I pick the team for next year."

Serena leaned in. "I understand you're being formal and all that, but come on. We both know my son is a shoo-in." She stood tall and brushed down the front of her apron. "Just let Toby know what night is good. Let me know if you need anything."

"This is going to be the longest few weeks of my life," Dax muttered. "Between the showcase tournament, looking through all the player information, and dealing with admissions, I'm going to need to stock up on my wine."

"I know the owner at the local winery. I can get you a good discount." Chablis winked.

Dax laughed.

They grew quiet as they dug into their meals.

For the next twenty minutes as they stuffed their faces, they kept the conversation light. They mostly talked about his sisters and her siblings. It was more like two old friends catching up, not two old lovers hashing out old problems.

She'd learned a lot about him and his feelings about their past. Much of how she felt about their relationship and their subsequent breakup made more sense to her, but she wondered if this conversation was finished.

"This was so good." He tossed his napkin to his plate. "Did you save room for dessert?"

"I couldn't eat another bite," she said. "I also need to get home. I have to be up at five. The drive to work is about forty minutes."

"How often do you work at the fire station?"

"It's always changing."

"Is it always twenty-four shifts?"

"No. Sometimes it's twelve, other times it's forty-eight. It all depends on where they need me. I'm kind of the swing girl now that I'm part time."

"How does your family—especially your mom—feel about you sticking with it?"

"Believe it or not, they are all supportive." She glanced at her watch. "I'm really sorry. I need get home. That alarm comes early." She dug into her purse. "If you can flag the waiter so I can pay—"

"This is my treat."

"I can't let you do that."

"You can. And you will," he said. "You can get the next one."

"Oh. That's sneaky." However, she was glad he brought it up. "How about I cook for you?"

He lowered his chin and raised both brows. "You learned how to make something other than hot dog on a stick over an open fire?"

"Har har. Aren't you the funny guy. Yes. How about Saturday after the parade? Do you have plans?"

"I do now." He stood when she did and took her by the biceps. He gave her a gentle kiss on the lips. "Thank you for tonight. I had a good time."

"So did I. I'll see you Saturday." She sidestepped him and did her best not to run to the parking lot. Once she found her car, she blew out a big breath.

Malbec was right. She had to tell him, but it wasn't going to be as easy as his confession.

4

DAX

Dax stood in front of the brewery on the outskirts of town. The building was on the opposite side of Main Street from all the major activities. The property surrounding the building used to be a farm. However, now it had been sliced up into different businesses serving the good people of Candlewood Falls.

He stared at the larger-than-life image of himself. He couldn't believe it. Axel had more than captured Dax's image, right down to the intensity in his eyes, which were currently burning as he stared at his hand holding the Stanley Cup.

One of his proudest moments in his career.

Even if it had been bittersweet because he hadn't a woman in his life that he really loved to share it with. It had been that moment that he realized how empty his life had been. He spent another six years and four

Stanley Cups pretending he was the happiest man on earth, when in reality, all he wanted was Chablis.

"That's fucking amazing, Axel," Dax said with thick emotion building in his throat.

"I have to agree," Raf, Axel's brother, said as he grabbed him in a brotherly hug.

"I took advantage of expression and added the water and all the background colors. The building needed a facelift anyway. But if you look, you can see several places where I included pieces of Dax's history. See there in the hockey stick?"

"Or in the top corner," Malbec said.

Dax took a step back. He did his best to listen to everyone's accolades about Axel's piece of artwork, but his emotions got the better of him. That part of his life was really over. He'd never hear the crowd roar for number seventeen again.

"I'm humbled," Dax said softly. "Thank you."

"I hope everyone in town likes it," Axel said.

"They will." Raf slapped his little brother on the back. "Don't you worry about that."

"Why don't we take this party inside," Brad said. "Dax is buying the first round."

"I am?"

"You bet your ass you are. You've got all that pro hockey money burning up your wallet." Brad put an arm around Dax's shoulders and let him into the brewery.

Everyone else followed.

Dax handed the bartender his credit card and told the bartender that the night was on him. Brad had a point. Not that he had money to throw away, but he did have more than most.

"How do you think Chablis is going to like looking at that image of you as she comes into town after working her other gig?" Caleb asked as he slid into the booth across from Dax. "Or have the two of you made up? Someone told me they saw you at dinner last night."

Back in the day, Caleb had been one of his best friends. Over the years, they'd lost touch, especially after Caleb had been accused of a crime he hadn't committed. Not because Dax believed it. He didn't. But because Caleb had left town and didn't speak to anyone.

"My sister's not going to care," Merlot said as he sat down next to Dax.

"Look who's still following around the big boys," Caleb joked. But he should be careful; Merlot might have given up being a parole officer, but rumor had it he was always packing.

"I know. It's so annoying to have my little brother follow me around like a pathetic puppy." Malbec set a round of shots on the table, along with four beers. "And now I have to work with him day in and day out. Along with my wife and my sister."

"Don't forget Mom." Merlot rolled his eyes.

Dax laughed. "Something tells me you all love it."

"I'm not complaining," Merlot said. "But seriously, you and my sister? What's going on?"

"Nothing." Dax lifted the shot of tequila. "To old friends."

Everyone else took their shots and raised them. They all tilted their heads and downed the liquid.

"You're not getting off the hook," Merlot said.

"Let it go." Malbec arched a brow.

If Dax wasn't up against the wall, he'd excuse himself, but then Malbec would have to move and it would be a scene and they would all think he was being defensive. Besides, he was wondering what the hell had gotten into the two brothers.

"Why? They went out. Was it a date?" Merlot asked.

"No," Dax finally got the chance to interject. "I wanted to clear the air about a few things and start fresh as friends."

"And did you do that?" Malbec asked.

"I believe so." Dax nodded.

"And did my sister?"

Dax cocked his head. "I don't like cryptic shit. Get to the point."

"I don't have one." Malbec stared at his beer, twisting and tugging at the label as if he had something to say, but couldn't find the words.

Dax had known Malbec a long time and even though he'd been a grade behind him in school, they'd been best friends long before Dax had fallen in love with his sister.

"What's going on?"

"Nothing," Malbec said.

"That's bullshit. You have this look like you and I have unfinished business. Is there something you need to get off your chest?"

"Whatever happened between you and my sister is between the two of you." Malbec lifted his gaze.

"You know something that I don't. What is it?"

"I don't believe that one dinner could clear up all the hurt that went on between the two of you."

"Maybe not, but it's a start." Dax decided it was time to drop the conversation. He didn't want to press Malbec at a bar during a party. Whatever bug he had up his ass could be dealt with in private another day.

"Oh, my God," Merlot said, breaking up the tension. "I can't believe my eyes. It's Luke Sheridan."

"Who?" Dax asked.

"You don't remember Luke?" Malbec asked. "He hung out some with Merlot. They got in trouble doing a little drag racing on the back roads outside of town."

"Oh yeah. Isn't he some kind of stuntman or some shit?" Dax asked.

"He is," Merlot said.

"What's he doing back in town?" Caleb asked.

"His sister is getting married. We're having it at the winery." Merlot slipped from the booth. "It's a bit over the top with some of the extra activities they are doing, but it's good for business." He tapped his knuckles on the table. "Excuse me. I'm going to go say hi to him. I'll be back in a bit."

Dax lifted his beer to his lips and took a long draw. He glanced around the bar, humbled by the turnout for a pre-unveiling of his mug shot. Granted, it was as much about Axel as it was about him, but still. His heart swelled. Being with this group again felt as though he'd never left.

"I can't believe you're going to be responsible for coaching young boys," Caleb said.

"I can't believe you got Brooklyn to agree to marry you," Dax said. "And without Brad beating the shit out of you."

Caleb laughed. "I'm a little surprised by both myself."

"And this one." Dax pointed a finger to Malbec. "Having a baby. When did we all get old?"

"Speak for yourself, has-been." Malbec slapped him on the shoulder.

A fiery flash on the television behind the bar caught Dax's attention. He pushed his way out of the booth and raced across the room. "Turn it up," he barked at the bartender.

"*The crash happened an hour ago. It involved two trucks carrying gasoline. The explosion occurred shortly after firefighters arrived at the scene. Five firefighters were injured and taken to the—*"

"Malbec. Merlot. Isn't that the county your sister works for?"

Malbec was at his side in seconds. "Yes," he said.

"Shit," Merlot mumbled. "I better call Mom. She's going to be freaking out."

Dax pulled out his cell and hit Chablis' contact information. "Straight to voicemail."

"I texted her," Malbec said. "We'll have to wait it out. They didn't say anyone was critical, so that's good."

"I'm calling the hospital." Dax slipped outside. He wasn't going to sit around and *wait it out*. He'd been doing that for seventeen years.

Chablis

Chablis tossed her keys on the table by her door. She had mild first-degree chemical burns on her arms and hands. She also had a concussion from being tossed backward during the explosion and hitting the pavement like a rag doll.

That hurt more than the burns.

"Thanks for bringing me home, Daddy."

"Are you sure you don't want me to stay with you?" Her father strolled into the kitchen and put away a few groceries and the casserole and treats her mom had whipped up for her.

"I'm just going to binge-watch *Below Deck* reruns and sleep. You hate that show."

"We could watch something else," her father suggested.

But the reality was she wanted to be alone so she could let the tears come. She'd never been so scared in her life. She'd fought some serious fires before. Dealt with some hard situations. But that explosion had been like nothing she ever witnessed before.

She could still hear it echoing between her ears. And the heat prickled her skin like a cattle prod. For the first time in her life, she thought she might die.

Curling her fingers around her father's strong biceps, she mustered up a smile. "I love you, Daddy. But it's one in the morning. Go home and be with Mom. I'll call you tomorrow."

"Okay. But will you promise me that you'll call me if you need anything? I'll leave my phone on all night. And tomorrow there isn't anything too pressing that I can't change my schedule to be with you."

"I promise."

He leaned in and kissed her cheek. "Follow the doctor's orders."

She looped her arm through his and guided him to the door. "Don't worry."

"It's a father's prerogative to do that." He pulled open the door. "Oh. Hello, Dax. Isn't it a little late for you to be showing up?"

"Hi, Carter," Dax said, holding a bouquet of flowers

in his hand. "I saw you pull in. I've been trying to reach Chablis since I heard what happened. I wanted to make sure she was okay."

"She's fine. It's late. Time for you to go home."

"Dad," Chablis said with a stern tone. "I'm not fourteen. You don't get to send him away like that."

Her father turned and glared.

"He's right." Dax handed her the flowers. "I'll call you—"

"This is ridiculous. Come in," she said. The need for tears was suddenly replaced with the desire for human contact.

And not her father's.

"Dad. Tell Mom thanks for the food. I'll call you in the morning."

"Why does this feel like déjà vu?" Her father tapped his temple. "Oh, I know why. I'm being ditched for the star hockey player. Again."

She laughed.

"In all seriousness," her father started. "She's been through a lot. Don't stay too late."

"I won't." Dax nodded.

She stood in the doorway and waited for her father to get in his car and turn the engine on before turning her attention to Dax. "You didn't have to come over. Or bring me these." She stuck her nose in the pretty bouquet. They smelled like a meadow on a sunny day. "They're beautiful."

"I would have waited until morning, but I saw you

pull in." He gently took her arm and lifted it. "That's got to hurt."

"It's all superficial burns. They aren't bad. But do you mind if we go sit? My head is pounding."

"Here. Let me help."

He took the flowers and practically ran into the kitchen where he found a vase.

She made herself comfortable on the sofa in the small family room and watched him skillfully cut the stems of the flowers and arrange them in the vase as if he were a master florist.

"Do you want something to drink? Water? Juice?" he asked.

"Water would be nice."

He brought her a glass and sat on the other side of the sofa, lifting her feet and resting them on his lap. Normally, she'd protest, but she didn't have the energy.

"How was the unofficial unveiling?" When she'd heard what Axel was doing, she'd been super annoyed. The last thing she wanted was to drive into town day in and day out and see her ex-boyfriend's face.

She still didn't.

But the town did and she understood why.

"I have to admit, I'm not sure how I feel about seeing myself on that building all the time, but Axel is an amazing artist."

"That he is," Chablis agreed.

"It's so weird to see all my old friends and listen to them talk about marriage and kids. On the one hand, being with them feels like I've been catapulted back to my youth. But on the other hand, it makes me feel old."

She rested her hand on her middle. It was hard not to think about what she'd done. It wasn't about regrets because she didn't regret the action.

Only the silence.

Dax had the right to know, and she should have told him seventeen years ago. It wouldn't have changed things. Not even if she'd known Traci wasn't his girlfriend. The fact remained they weren't ready for each other.

Or being parents.

"Neither one of us are old."

"I feel like I'm too old to start a family."

"Do you want one?" she asked. "I mean, Malbec is having his first kid soon and they plan on more. Caleb is your age and he and Brooklyn plan on kids."

He placed his hand on her foot and rubbed. It was something he used to do when they were dating. Whenever they would be talking about something or mindlessly watching TV, his hands would always go to her feet. She never minded.

And she didn't now.

"I didn't mean to get into a deep conversation. That's the last thing you need."

He was right about that, and she was grateful for the opportunity to switch gears.

"I take it you're going to have to take some time off work?" he asked.

"A few weeks from the fire station and I don't know how long my folks are going to make me stay away from the winery."

"I've got an idea."

"Oh. That's scary," she said.

"This weekend and all next week I'm recruiting. How would you like to come with me? We can watch some of the games together. You can check out different ones. You can give me your perspective on the kids on the ice. You've always had such great insight into the game."

"You really want my opinion?"

He nodded. "I have a list of twenty-seven kids that have applied. I have five spots open. Only one kid do I know I want to take. It's really hard because there are so many games to watch and they're kids and they know I'm there. Once they see me, or their parents do, they act differently."

"So, you want me to be your eyes when you're watching a different game."

"Exactly," he said.

"What about Serena and Toby? They will know I'm there and they will have something to say about it."

"I'm allowed to have independent eyes and you're not making decisions. Just giving me advice. Besides, they don't have to know why you're there." He winked.

She cocked her head. "Don't give those two something to talk about. This town is already buzzing about what may or may not happen between you and me."

"I hear there's a pool down at the brewery," he said with a laugh.

She kicked him. "There better not be, but if there is, I'll take one hundred to one that there isn't."

"Ouch. That hurt."

"What? The kick in the thigh or the statement?" She smiled.

"Both, but back to hockey," he said. "I'll send you to games that TJ won't be at so you won't run into Serena or Toby. I'll give you a list of things I want you to note."

"I'm not a hockey player."

"But you know the game," he said. "You used to critique me after every single one of my games and you were always on point. Come on. Please. It will be fun and it will give you something to do. I know how much you hate to be idle."

"Doc says I have to lay low tomorrow, so probably can't do it until after the parade on Saturday."

"No worries. I can handle tomorrow on my own and I'm not going on Saturday."

She smiled. "Okay. But on one condition."

"What's that?"

"You buy me a funnel cake every day."

"Deal." He squeezed her ankle. "On that note, I should let you get some rest. I wouldn't be surprised if your dad is sitting out in the driveway waiting for me to leave." He stood, placing her foot on the sofa. "Don't get up. I'll see myself out." He leaned over and tucked a piece of her hair behind her ear and stared into her eyes for a long moment.

She held her breath, waiting for him to say good night. But instead, he brushed his lips tenderly across her mouth in a sweet, loving kiss. It wasn't the kind of kiss shared between friends. A spark deep in her gut tried to roar to a flame, but she squelched it. She couldn't allow this to deepen. It was too much. Too soon. So many emotions raced through her mind. She couldn't think straight.

"Sleep well."

She clutched her pendant and remained breathlessly on the sofa. She heard the door open, then shut. She brought her fingers to her lips. Everything she felt for Dax in the past had been brought to the present. Nothing had changed. Her love for him was as strong as ever.

And the secret she carried still darkened her soul.

5

DAX

Dax gave up sleeping around four thirty in the morning. He'd changed into workout clothes and went for a run.

But that didn't help.

His best-laid plan to slowly woo Chablis was quickly going to shit. About the only place Dax had any patience was on the ice. He'd always been known for his ability to read the ice. To see things that no one else could. On power plays, he'd pass until the right shot came into view. On penalty kills, he'd keep his cool, knowing that it wasn't about chasing the puck, but shutting down lanes. It was never about being a star. His goal was to get the job done.

To win.

As a team.

When it came to Chablis, he was not only flying solo, but he was flying blind. He knew the young version of her, but the adult Chablis was a bit of a mystery. She'd matured. She'd always been a bit of an introvert, but now she was guarded. However, maybe she'd always been like that and he'd been too selfish to pick up on it.

He strolled around the back of the winery like Malbec told him to and knocked on the employee door.

"Hey," Malbec said as he pushed open the door. "I was surprised to hear from you this early."

"Couldn't sleep," he admitted.

"Do you mind going for a walk through the vineyard?"

"Not at all." Dax followed him down the windy path toward the river's edge. The sun had begun to show itself, warming the dark sky with its light. This had always been Dax's favorite part of the day. It was when he did his best thinking.

Of course, it was usually about Chablis.

"How's Eliza Jane feeling?" Dax asked.

"Fat." Malbec laughed. "And those are her words, not mine. Personally, I think she's never been sexier, but I say that and she thinks I'm full of shit."

"I'm sure it's all hormones."

"Oh. Don't ever say that to a pregnant lady. Not unless you want to have a wall of pillows between you when you sleep." Malbec ran a hand across the top of his head. "She's really uncomfortable lately and I feel like all I do is say the wrong thing. I've resorted to asking both Riesling and my mother for advice."

"You're asking *the Weezer* for advice on how to handle a woman? Wow. Talk about the world flipping upside down."

"I know, right?"

They took a turn down the first row of vines. It smelled like a combination of fresh grapes and fine wines.

"So, speaking of needing a little insight. What brings you by at six in the morning?"

"Your sister." Dax stuffed his hands in his pockets and stared at the rising sun.

"What about her?"

"I'm going to dive right in and not hold anything back. If that's okay," Dax said.

"Please."

"I thought I could come back here and start off slow. I mean, there was a world of hurt between me and Chablis. But I showed up at her place last night."

Malbec paused in the middle of the path. "Are you okay?" He looked at Dax with what could only be described as pity in his eyes.

"Shouldn't you be asking if she's okay?" Dax asked.

"Well, yes. But you're the one here talking to me, so I thought maybe something happened between the two of you."

"Does this have to do with that statement you made last night at the brewery?"

Malbec raised his hands. "There are things in my sister's life that only she can tell you."

"Come on, man. That's bullshit. What is it that I should know about Chablis? Is it about that guy she was engaged to?"

"I'm sorry I brought it up. I spoke out of turn. You've been back in town for only a couple of days. Give her a chance to get used to that. She'll tell you when she's ready." Malbec waved out his hand and continued walking. "What is it that you wanted to discuss with me? And remember, don't hold anything back."

Dax chuckled. Leave it to Malbec to toss his words back at him. "I wasn't truthful when I said all I wanted to do was clear the air and be friends. I wanted to set the stage so I could start things up again."

"You think I don't know that?" Malbec paused in front of one of the vines and checked out some of the grapes. "I saw the way you were looking at her when you waltzed into the gift shop. Everyone did. And the entire town has been talking about it."

"That's an exaggeration."

"Not really." Malbec waved his hand out in front and moved toward the next row of grapes.

Dax had grown up listening to Malbec discuss grapes and the wine-making process, but he knew shit about it.

"You both moved back within a few months of each other and she's renting on the property you own. That makes people wonder."

"Wonderful," Dax mumbled. He already felt like he

was living in a fishbowl with his professional life; now he had to with his personal one too? "Look. I don't know what to do. I don't want to fuck this up. Right now, I've got her helping me at the rink."

"She loves hockey. She'll enjoy that and you'll be able to spend some time together."

"That was the point. But it's not romantic."

Malbec laughed. "Since when has my sister ever been romantic."

"We're not kids anymore and I want to sweep her off her feet. Show her I'm not the same stupid idiot that told her to go running back to mommy."

"Why don't you just tell her how you feel? And then take her on a date without the pretext of it being to clear the air. Go bowling. She still enjoys that. Or apple picking. Hell, take her to see Faith."

"Who the hell is Faith?"

"That's Sam Wilde's girl. She's a fortune-teller."

Dax couldn't contain the laughter. "Little science boy is dating someone who reads tarot cards? This I have to see."

"According to her, I'm going to have a daughter. Eliza Jane told me if that happens, we're not allowed to nickname her Weezer, like my mom wants."

"You know I'm going to call her Little Weez because I can."

"You call my child that and I will hurt you," Malbec said. "But my point was if you come at Chablis under the idea you only want to be friends and then make a move, she's going to reject you. But if you tell her that you still have feelings for her and then take her out, she's going to be more receptive."

"I don't know. Whenever she would break up with me, it was like she'd flipped a switch in her mind and her heart."

"She gets that from my mom. As kids we watched our mother do that to our dad. And to us kids. My mother could be hugging us one second and teaching us a life lesson a second later. And some of those life lessons weren't conventional."

"I remember." Dax had never really been afraid of Weezer, but he never wanted to be on her bad side. He knew that Chablis' parents liked him and respected his family. If they hadn't, he would have never been allowed to spend the time he did with the family. He had Sunday dinners. Sleepovers. And they all came to his games. But the way Weezer carried herself kept the world at a distance and the older Chablis got, the more she'd picked up on that trait. Now that Dax could look back on that time in his life, he could see that he used that to make sure he pushed Chablis away. He did small subtle things to show her that hockey would always be his first love.

Not her.

And while that was only partially true, he hated that he'd hurt her when she'd come to Buffalo. He should have been honest. He should have told her that hockey was his priority and that he knew for the next ten to twenty years, depending on how his career went, a family wasn't going to be in his future.

"It's been a long time since you and Chablis were a couple." Malbec stopped at the edge of the vineyard. The sun had appeared in the sky, casting a bright-yellow glow.

"Yeah, but my heart doesn't see it that way." Dax tapped his chest. "Every time I stepped out onto that ice, every freaking game, I glanced to the stands and pretended she was there, watching, cheering me on."

"She was in a strange way because she watched every single game. If you're worried she doesn't care about you, then stop. She does."

"I get that. But we have a long history that dates back to grade school, and caring for someone isn't the same as wanting to try again." Dax inhaled sharply. The familiar scent of grapes calmed his nerves. He always enjoyed walking the vineyards. "I kissed her last night."

"Dude. Even that is too much information. That's my sister." Leave it to Malbec to always try to lighten the mood. "But that's a start."

"She was hesitant to commit. It was like she only half participated."

"Well, she might have been a little out of it. My dad did say they gave her some painkillers."

"She wasn't taking them by the time I saw her," Dax said. "I know Chablis and the way she kissed me like she used to right before she dumped me."

"Oh. I see," Malbec said. "Maybe you caught her off

guard. Or maybe she was tired. Or maybe you need to be talking to her, and not standing in this vineyard yapping with me."

Malbec had a good point. "You really think I should just tell her I want to try again?"

"Yes."

"Just blurt it out."

"Oh, my God, Dax. We're not in high school anymore. You're a grown man." Malbec glanced at his watch. "She's an early riser. Text her or give her a call and bring her some breakfast. She still loves pancakes and bacon."

"I do make a mean breakfast." Dax smiled. His old friend was right. The worst that could happen was that he was rejected out of the gate and that wasn't going to change things.

That was only going to make him work harder to prove he was worthy of her love.

Chablis

Chablis padded from her bedroom to the kitchen, surprised she'd slept through the night. She'd expected the pain from her burns to wake her up.

Or a killer headache.

Neither happened.

Though her arms throbbed and her head had a slow pound that she hoped would be calmed by a tall mug of caffeine.

Her nostrils tickled with the scent of sizzling bacon.

But how could that be?

Perhaps it was simply wishful thinking. Unless maybe her mother or father had shown up with her favorite breakfast.

She rounded the corner from the hallway to the small U-shaped kitchen and stopped dead in her tracks.

Dax stood in front of her stove wearing a pair of gym shorts, a T-shirt, and an apron while he flipped a pancake.

"What the hell are you doing?"

"What does it look like?" He handed her a fresh mug of coffee.

"Breaking and entering. I should call the police." She lifted the cup to her nose and inhaled sharply. God, that smelled good. She blew on the dark liquid before taking a small sip.

Freaking delicious.

"That's a bit dramatic, don't you think?"

"Nope. I realize you're my landlord, but I don't appreciate you using your key to enter my house whenever you feel like it."

He took down a couple of plates and loaded them up with food. "I tried texting and calling. You didn't answer. I knocked. You didn't answer. I was worried. So I called your dad. He gave me permission to enter."

That's what she got for not checking her phone. "Doesn't make me feel better. Please tell me you didn't go into my bedroom."

"I only peeked when you didn't answer and once I saw you were blissfully asleep, I waited until I heard the water running before I started breakfast."

She squeezed his shoulder. "You have not changed, but my father certainly has. Remember when he came racing over to my mom's house at one in the morning to make sure we were staying on opposite ends of the house?"

He set the plates on the table and sat across from her. "Like it was yesterday, but in your father's defense, I was eighteen and you weren't seventeen yet. I had returned for a long weekend from Canada. Not to mention I had literally just snuck out of your room when he showed up. If he'd come five minutes earlier, we might have gotten caught."

"They knew we were dating." Chablis doused the pancakes with butter and syrup. "What did my mother think when she said it was fine for you to spend the night?"

"Exactly what we told her. That we broke up because I went away."

Chablis laughed. "No one bought that, especially my mother."

"They were just looking out for their little girl." Dax dug into his food like it was the last supper. Of course, breakfast had always been his favorite, especially all the foods his trainers wouldn't allow him to eat, so when he got the chance to have them, he went a little nuts.

Like he did with the six pancakes she counted and the six pieces of bacon to match.

For the next few minutes she watched him attack his food and guzzle his coffee while she sat back and nibbled at hers. She should be super annoyed by his presence and tell him to leave, but she wasn't. If she were being honest with herself, she hadn't been looking forward to spending the day by herself since she'd been forced into taking medical leave from both jobs.

She glanced at the bandages on her arm. Her skin prickled with a slow burn. When the explosion happened and she saw the fire rip through her clothing before she'd had the chance to put on her suit, for the first time since she'd become a firefighter, she'd panicked. It only lasted a few seconds, but that terror was something she never wanted to experience again.

"Do you mind if I ask you something personal?" Dax asked.

"I guess not."

Dax had been the first boy she'd ever kissed. The first young man to see her naked. To touch her body. And the first man she'd slept with.

Didn't get any more personal than that.

"Why didn't you ever marry or have children?" Last night this topic had come up and she thought she'd dodged the conversation. It was never easy for her to discuss and it wasn't a simple answer. She could lie to him and give him the standard response that she told everyone that dared to ask.

Or she could be honest.

Neither one of them was ready for that.

Maybe she could come up with something in the middle.

"It took me some time getting over you," she admitted. "After I left you in Buffalo, I came back to Candlewood Falls and packed my things. I drove to Granger, where I went to firefighter school. I worked as much as I could and when I wasn't working, I was traveling."

"Where did you go?"

"Anywhere and everywhere. Mostly in the United States, but I took a few trips to Europe," she said.

"You did all that to get over our breakup?"

"It started out that way," she admitted. "But then I really fell in love with traveling. I had a couple of relationships before I met Brett and some them enjoyed it too, but none of them I could see myself marrying."

"But you felt differently about Brett?" Dax wiped his hands with his napkin and pushed his plate aside.

"At first, absolutely. He was kind and generous. Our only problem was with my family, but he had a point. Malbec and my mother were still at odds and I only added fuel to that fire. Add the problems that Riesling was going through with her ex and it was a recipe for disaster."

"Why? I don't understand."

"What I didn't know about Brett was that he cut his father and stepmother out of his life. He never talked about them. When I asked about his father, he told me he was dead, but he was alive and well and living in Upstate New York."

"Damn. That's cruel."

"I'm not going to get into why he cut his father out. That's not my story to tell, but he was tired of listening to me bitch about my family. After we broke up, I kind of gave up on the whole concept."

"I can understand why," Dax said.

"What about you? I mean, I saw you in the media with lots of women."

He rolled his eyes. "My way of getting over you, but it didn't work out so well for me. I'm not sure I ever did."

She swallowed. She wanted to ask him what he meant, but she had to believe he was teasing. "Har har. Aren't you the funny guy."

"I'm not kidding," he said. "I told myself that I was playing the field because I didn't when I was young. Then it became because I watched all my friends get married and then get divorced. It was always messy. But I realized that while I loved my life and I loved my career, I wasn't whole. You see, I never stopped loving you."

She pushed her chair back and jumped to her feet. "Don't you dare flip-flop from the other night. All you wanted was to clear the air. Start over as friends. You never said anything about still loving me."

"You're right. I didn't." He leaned back and lifted his chin.

"Furthermore, you went on about how it was best that we broke up and went our separate ways. That you were never totally committed to our relationship."

He nodded. "Again. You're right. But nowhere in that statement did I ever say I never loved you."

Her heart hammered in her throat. "What the hell are you saying, Dax?"

"That I don't want to be just friends," he said matter-of-factly. "I want to start over. I want us to date again."

"You got to be freaking kidding me right now." She turned and paced in a circle in the small kitchen while chewing on her fingernail. "Being your friend I can handle. Going to the rink and being a creeper while watching a bunch of adolescent boys play hockey and fucking with Toby and Serena sounds like a damn blast. But getting back together? That's a big leap. It's been seventeen years."

"I don't expect us to pick up where we left off. That would be impossible."

"No shit." She paused and snagged her coffee. She found the Baileys and twisted off the cap, pouring a double shot.

"Not to be a weirdo, but should you be drinking that? Aren't you taking pain meds or something?"

"Nope." She waved the bottle. "Want some?"

"No. I'm good."

Chablis took a sip. Her heart hammered in her chest. She felt like she was thirteen again and her brother was annoyed because Dax was more interested in her and not playing video games.

"All I'm asking for is a couple of real dates."

"You should have asked me that before declaring how much you think you still care for me," she mumbled. This should excite her. Instead, it utterly terrified her. She had the same feelings and being with him would be amazing.

But feelings didn't equate a happily ever after, because if it did, they would have spent the last seventeen years together.

Love had never been their problem.

Putting each other first had been.

She couldn't fault him for wanting his career and how could he deny her one either? Of course, she did things for her family, but still, making wine was something she was passionate about. Her family business had been something she desired. When Malbec left for California and her mother wouldn't give her a chance in taking his position, it was the equivalent of Dax never being drafted to the NHL.

While the world thought she'd chosen to study viticulture in college because that's what had been expected of her, she'd done it because her world revolved around the wine business. Everyone in

Candlewood Falls thought her mother was a little left of normal, but Chablis had adored and admired her mom. Chablis wanted to be just like her and stepping into her shoes in the winery would have been the biggest honor.

"I didn't mean to make you uncomfortable." He stood and cleared the table.

She leaned against the counter and sipped her coffee, letting the Baileys slide down her throat with ease.

"We had planned on you cooking me dinner tomorrow night after the parade, but instead, why don't we hang out in town. Grab a burger at the diner and maybe go to the movies."

"There's that new release... um..." She tapped her temple. "...I can't think of the name, but it's about a shipwreck and ghosts and it looks creepy."

"I know you love creepy." He rolled up his sleeves and began doing the dishes.

She wasn't about to stop him from doing those.

"If we do this dating thing, we're going to take it slow. You're not going to tell me you have deep feelings anymore. There will be no jumping into my bed on the first date. Much less the second one."

"You can set all the ground rules you want as long as we get to spend time together and kissing is involved and maybe a little bit of touching." He held up his finger and thumb.

She tried not to smile, but her mouth curled

upward. Her heart lurched to the back of her throat as he caught her gaze. He picked up the dish towel and dried his hands before sauntering in her direction.

He took her mug, took a sip, and set it on the counter. Taking her hands in his, he placed them gently on his shoulders. He wrapped his arms around her waist and heaved her against his chest.

She grunted. "We're not on a date," she managed with a raspy breath.

His fingers dug into her back and she arched. His tongue stroked across his full lips in a broad stroke before he took her mouth in a hot, wet kiss. "No. We're not," he whispered. "But it is the proper way to say goodbye to the girl I'm dating."

Her stomach flipped and flopped. She couldn't believe she'd agreed to this entire scenario.

"I better get going. I have about five hockey games to watch today."

"Sounds like fun." She walked him to the door.

He pressed his lips against her temple before he turned and headed toward his car.

For a long moment, she stood there, watching him drive away with her fingers tracing a path across her mouth. Going out with Dax was about the craziest thing she could think of doing.

Especially when she was keeping the kind of secret that would tear them apart.

Again.

. . .

Weezer

There was a lot to do before the parade on Saturday and the River Winery had offered to do a fair share of the planning and brunt some of the costs.

Weezer had no problem giving back to the community, especially when honoring such a fine young man as Dax Fabion.

She stepped from behind her desk in her office at the winery above the gift shop. Stepping onto the ledge, she looked down below. The room bustled with people coming and going. Over the years, she loved standing in this spot and watching townspeople come in to shop in her store, only it had been bittersweet because her children had all scattered.

Now, as she scanned the room, her son Merlot stood near the entrance to the wine tasting room, chatting with his old buddy, Luke Sheridan and Brielle Wilde, who were in town for a local wedding. She had no idea what Luke and Brielle wanted, since they weren't the bride and groom, but Merlot could handle it.

She smiled. A year ago, she wouldn't have been able to step back and allow anyone but herself to handle a special event.

Now, her daughter-in-law, Eliza Jane, headed up the wine-making department with the help of Chablis while Malbec ran the vineyard with Merlot's help. Although, Merlot was better suited in management.

Soon, Zinfandel would be brought on to work the books, and then Weezer would have to talk the twins into quitting their sales jobs so they could work full-time sales for the family.

It was all coming together, even though it was a good fifteen or so years later than planned.

The front door of the gift shop swung open and in walked Carter. He wore his work boots, jeans, and a standard dark T-shirt. He was still as sexy as the day she'd met him back when they were teenagers. She smiled and waved before turning and making her way down the windy staircase.

He greeted her at the bottom with a big hug and the kind of kiss that should be kept to the bedroom. "Hello, dear," he said.

"What brings you by?" Now that they were living together again, it seemed odd to have him stop by the winery randomly on days he was working at the law office.

"I can't come in and see my bride when I want to?"

"We're not married anymore, remember?"

"That's a technicality. One I'd like to change."

She laughed. "Let's not upset the balance too much. Besides, the town has enough to talk about as it is with Dax and Chablis. You should hear all the ridiculous things people are saying about them and why they broke up and if they are back together. It's crazier than the two of us."

"Do I want to know?"

"Probably not," she admitted. "But there is something that disturbs me."

"What's that?" Carter took her by the hand and led her to the side hallway and out of the way of customers.

"I overheard Alison Weatherby—"

"Serena Tillman's mother?" Carter interjected.

"Yes. Anyway. She was at the beauty parlor this morning and I overheard her chatting with her daughter about something she knew in Chablis' past that could really hurt Dax."

"I can't imagine what that would be," Carter said.

"Me neither, but we both know there are things we don't know about what happened in their relationship. Like she went to him when he first went to Buffalo after Malbec went to California, but Dax turned her away."

"I know." Carter palmed her cheek. "There's nothing that a gossip like Alison can do to hurt our kids. And all Serena wants is for her kid to make the team. Chablis told me Serena was all over Dax at the restaurant. She said it was totally embarrassing."

"That right there is cause for concern. Her husband, Toby, did some pretty shitty things to Dax back in the day. Dorothy told me that Toby went as far as to damage skate blades before tryouts and key games."

"That wasn't Toby," Carter said. "That was Serena."

Weezer tilted her head. "Seriously?"

"I remember all that transpired back in the day. Toby lived in Dax's shadow and he resented it. He acted like spoiled child and said and did a lot of stupid things on and off the ice. He got his girlfriend in on it too. But Dax is the one that had a career with the NHL. Not Toby."

Weezer dropped her head to Carter's chest. "Did we make the right decisions when it came to Chablis and Dax? I mean, I loved watching that boy's career, but we totally fucked with their relationship."

"If they wanted to be together back then, they would have defied us at all costs." Carter tilted her chin. "Malbec left home. That took some balls on his part. Riesling ran off and eventually so did Chablis. Merlot did his thing. It took us four kids to learn to let our children make their own decisions in life."

"Yeah, and the last three still ended up working away from the winery."

"But they are coming back without us having to beg them," Carter said.

"I'm worried." She let out a slow breath. "Of all our kids, I know Chablis the least. She could have a big skeleton in her closet and I would hate for that little bitch, Serena, to bring it out and wave it in front of Dax, especially when he showed up there last night with flowers."

"That was sweet," Carter said. "And he's there now making her breakfast."

Weezer tapped the center of her chest. "Those two deserve a second chance at love."

"I couldn't agree more." Carter kissed her nose. "However, we can't interfere. You have to promise me you'll leave them alone."

"You know I'm not going to do that." She cocked her head. "But I can promise I'll make a minimal nuisance of myself."

"That's fair. But as far as whatever games Serena and her mother might play, stay out of it. You getting in the middle of that shit show is only going to make it worse."

"Come on. Aren't you the least bit curious as to what dirt they think they have on our precious daughter?"

"Of course. But not enough to breathe life into it. Don't go poking the bear unless you want the bear to fight back."

She hated it when Carter made sense, which was most of the time. If she tried to find out what Serena and Alison were talking about, she might end up bringing a rumor to light and hurting her own daughter in the process.

That wouldn't be good.

"Maybe you could ask Chablis about it," Weezer said. "She confides in you a lot more than me."

"Oh no." Carter shook his head. "I'm happy to play

matchmaker and invite them both over to dinner and that kind of thing. But I'm not going to—oh hell." He cupped the back of Weezer's neck and kissed her forehead. "The things I do for you."

"Thank you, honey."

"You're welcome, dear," he said. "But I'm expecting to have my favorite for dinner tonight."

"Of course." She smiled. "I'll even bake an apple pie."

"Now you're talking," he said. "I better get back to the office. I'll see you around six."

She kissed her husband. Well, not legally, but in every way that mattered. She watched him saunter through the gift shop. Carter had stood by her through some difficult times and she knew she was damn lucky to have him at her side.

"Merlot," she called. "I'm leaving for the day."

"What?" Her son raced to her side. "Are you feeling okay?"

"I'm fine. You don't need me here today. I'm leaving you in charge of the booth for the parade. All the information is on my laptop in my office."

"Are you sure you're not sick?" Merlot touched the back of his hand to her forehead.

"I'm going to go home and cook dinner for your father. I'm making his favorite and a pie. That is going to take all day."

"Can I come over?"

She patted her son's cheek. "Your dad and I might get a little frisky, so come at your own risk."

"Ew. Gross, Ma."

Weezer laughed. However, before she went home, she would need to stop by the orchard and buy some apples. That meant going past the garden club where she suspected that Alison would be in attendance since she only worked part-time at the abortion clinic a few towns over.

6

DAX

Dax sat in the back of the stands with his large hot chocolate, a turkey sandwich, and a clipboard. He wished he didn't have to watch this game, but three kids that wanted to attend CFW Prep were going to be on the ice.

One of them happened to be TJ Tillman.

There were six other coaches from other prep schools in the stands with him, all looking at different kids.

Some might even be looking at the same players since it wasn't unheard of for children to apply to more than one school.

Dax had sent his application to three schools, but he'd had his heart set on CFW Prep. Not only because it had a great hockey program, but because he'd only be fifteen minutes from Chablis.

He'd been a freshman when they had started dating

and she'd been in eighth grade, as crazy as that sounded, but from the moment he had his first kiss, he knew she was the only girl he wanted to spend time with.

The only girl he'd be willing to risk getting in trouble for.

The only girl he'd let wear his jersey.

His phone buzzed. He lifted it. A few emails had come through and one of them was from the division one school in Massachusetts.

They were interested.

He was only interested if Chablis didn't want him in her life. But he'd go through the motions of taking the interview. He had to. Of course, that meant he'd end up leaving CFW Prep after only one year of coaching, but he hoped that wouldn't be the case.

If he could win over Chablis, he'd stay.

The Zamboni finished cleaning the ice and the two teams skated to their respective benches.

Dax took a bite of his sandwich while he scanned the players numbers, checking off the three players.

TJ and William were on the same team, while Eddie was on the opposing team. All three young men were thirteen and going to be freshmen in the fall. They were all good players, though Eddie stood out the most.

"Hey. Aren't you Dax Fabion?" one of the other coaches asked.

"In the flesh." He glanced over his shoulder.

"I thought that was you." The man moved down two bleacher rows. "I don't know if you remember me or not, but I'm Jim Dino."

"Holy shit. Yeah. We played together on a couple elite travel teams up in Canada." He held out his hand. "Are you coaching?"

"Head coach for Gerling Prep in Upstate."

"They have a good program, I hear."

"I'd like to think so," Jim said. "I couldn't believe it when I heard you were going to be coaching. I thought it was a weird rumor or something."

"Nope. It's true."

"Do you mind me asking why?"

"Not at all." Dax had been asked this question so many times he started to find it amusing. "I was ready to retire and I was also ready to come home."

"That's right. You went to CFW Prep."

Dax nodded. "My sisters and parents live here." He wanted to say the woman he loved more than life itself had brought him back, but he figured that would be over the top and Chablis wouldn't have appreciated it anyway.

"Why not coach college? Or get into broadcasting?"

"I wanted to be here," Dax said. "Besides, my degree is actually in education, if you can believe that."

"I forgot you waited to turn pro until you finished college." Jim set this clipboard on his lap and flipped over a page. "I signed with an NHL team after college, but I never got called up from the farm team. After a few years of that, my wife and I had our first kid and I decided it was time to move on. I had a good run, but I was always on the cusp, you know?"

"It's not easy. Sometimes I think I got lucky. Right place. Right time."

Jim slapped him on the back. "No. You had mad skills. And you had a work ethic second to none."

"I appreciate that," Dax said.

"So, who are you looking at?"

"Tillman, Hook, and March," Dax admitted just as the ref dropped the puck.

TJ was the center and he pushed the puck back to his defenseman, which was a good move. On the ice with him was Willman Hook, who was his right wing. Hook was a decent player, but since Tillman almost never passed, it was hard to know how good.

The defenseman dumped the puck across the blue line and both Hook and Tillman raced for it. Hook was playing his position. Tillman was not.

Tillman came away with it and circled the net.

Williams was open, but Tillman didn't pass. Instead, he shot. He missed, and the other team ended up skating to the other end and scored.

"I coach a summer program and both Hook and Tillman have been through it. They are both talented players, but as you can see, Tillman is selfish and that's more because of his father."

"I played with Toby at CFW Prep."

"Oh, shit. I didn't think about that," Jim said. "I'm

glad Tillman didn't apply to my school, but Hook did and I'll be honest, he's on my short list. But I have to admit, it surprises me because Hook and Tillman are often a package deal."

"Hook is more middle of the road for me. However, March, on the other team, is one of my top picks."

"Damn. You're lucky. That kid is good. I heard he only applied to like four schools."

"So far, I'm impressed by what I've seen," Dax said. "But why are Hook and Tillman a two for one deal?"

"The moms are besties, I guess. They always take lessons together. When they've switched travel teams, they did it together. I will say, Tillman and Hook usually play better, but TJ's still a lone wolf," Jim said. "What are you going to do about TJ? I know I'd cut him if he was trying out for me and in your shoes, that would suck."

"I don't know yet. The boy has a lot of potential but I'm not ready to make any decisions about anyone." Dax couldn't afford to discuss TJ in great detail with anyone. Not that he didn't feel as though he could trust Jim, but the reality was that he didn't know the man. Besides, Dax knew he had to do what was best for the team.

And the school.

"No amount of potential would make me willingly want to deal with TJ's parents. I was nervous he would apply and when I got the list, I was so relieved. I hear he's a good student, so he's not borderline when it comes to his grades."

"Straight A's. So, admissions will accept him no problem, but he won't get a dorm room unless I say yes to him on the team. No scholarship unless I say yes. And I know his parents; he won't go if he doesn't make it."

"That's absolutely true," Jim said. "I know Toby wants his kid to go to CFW really bad. So does his wife." Jim jotted a couple things down on his clipboard as two players got into a tiff on the ice, sending them both to the penalty box.

Dax remembered Toby's father being a pain in the ass when they were kids. Charlie Tillman started off as an assistant coach, but soon none of the head coaches wanted him on the bench because of the way he behaved. Charlie would stand in the corner and bang on the plexiglass, yelling at all the children about what they were doing wrong.

Never what they did right.

And it was always about how everyone made his son look bad.

Especially Dax.

Toby was different. He didn't yell at the other kids. And he didn't tell his son he sucked. But he did make a fuss over the decisions the coaches made. And he did tell his kid he was great, even when he made mistakes.

However, today he chose to sit quietly in the stands by himself.

Watching this game, especially now that his son's team was down by two goals, had to be killing Toby. TJ's current level of play was hurting the team. TJ had one thing on his mind and that was his himself. Every time he got the puck, he tried to score himself. He wanted the goal. The glory. Instead of the points.

That wasn't a good look.

That's not how a man made a team or built a career and that meant Toby had learned nothing from his own life.

But a child shouldn't suffer from the sins of a father, if the child was teachable.

Time to find out.

"I'll be back." Dax stood.

"Oh. You're seriously not going to go make a request between periods, are you?"

"Do me a favor and watch Toby's reaction." Dax jogged down the bleachers and made his way around to the bench. He waited for the end of the first period before strolling behind the players.

"Coach Fabion," one the other coaches greeted him while the boys shuffled past him into the locker room between periods. "It's a pleasure."

"The pleasure's all mine." Dax held out his hand. "I was wondering if we could chat for a second."

"Sure thing." The coach stepped to the side. The Zamboni made its way onto the ice to clean it between periods.

Dax would never forget the day the CFW Prep did

this to him during tryouts. He flipped his line upside down and put him with one of the weaker players on the team. Dax always liked playing with the other boy, but it was often hard to play by his coach's passing rules when this kid didn't skate half as hard or as fast as Dax. What Dax didn't understand was this had nothing to do with him, and everything to do with the other boy and Toby.

Right now, Dax needed to separate TJ from Hook. There was no way Dax would ever see Hook's potential if he was always on the same line. But also, he needed to see how TJ would handle being without his wingman. Without the one kid whom Toby would occasionally pass to.

"Would you be willing to pull Hook off Tillman's line for the next period? It doesn't matter to me which line Hook plays on, just not Tillman's. Oh, and I'd like see Hook play center."

"Is that because you're looking at TJ or Hook?"

"I'm looking at both, but I can't get a good assessment on Hook."

The coach rubbed the back of his neck. "I know this game isn't going my way right now, but that's my line. Normally those boys work better together. Or at least Hook does. TJ's trying to show off because of all you prep school coaches. We're going to talk to him. Actually, Hook is talking with him now. They're close. TJ will settle down."

"I'm just asking for one period. The outcome of

this game doesn't mean anything, but the playing time and performance does. Right now, both TJ and Hook are on the chopping block with all the coaches out there. We don't want that. They both have enormous potential. However, to see it, we need to separate them."

"You're right," the coach nodded. "However, be prepared for the wrath of Toby Tillman. He won't be happy."

"I used to play with Toby. Trust me. I can handle him." Dax hoped. "Thanks. I really appreciate this, but I have one more favor."

"What's that?"

"Mind if I have a little chat with both Hook and TJ as they come out?" While it was more than frowned upon for the parents to talk to the coaches, there was nothing out there that said the coaches couldn't have conversations with the kids.

"It's your funeral with their parents." The coach shrugged.

Dax waited with his hands stuffed in his pockets for about eight minutes before the team shuffled out of the locker room.

"Hook. TJ. I need to speak with you," he said, waving his hand.

Both boys glanced up.

Hook paused with wide eyes. "Um. Yes, sir." He scurried over.

"Wait right there, TJ. I'll be with you in a second."

Dax didn't want to have the boys hear each other's conversation.

TJ nodded as he gripped his stick. He glanced toward the stands.

Dax assumed at his father, but he didn't have the inclination to look.

"I take it you know who I am," Dax started.

"Only one of the greatest hockey players to ever play," Hook said.

Dax enjoyed the compliment. "I'm also the new coach for CFW Prep and I've asked your coach to make some changes. I'd like to see you play on a different line. Without TJ."

Hook's mouth twitched into a smile.

Dax could tell he tried not to.

"I'm not sure who your coach is going to put you with, but I really want to see what you're capable of."

"Yes, sir."

"All right. Go out there and have fun."

Hook nodded and took off for the bench.

TJ slowly made his way over to Dax. "Yeah, Coach?" he said.

"Tough game so far."

"We'll come back."

"I'd like to see that," Dax said. "But I'd also like to see you play with some other teammates."

TJ jerked his head. "You're changing my line? I'm sorry, Coach, but I don't think that's a good idea. Hook and I are the best on the team. We need to be together."

Dax found that statement interesting.

And telling.

Because the few games he'd seen, TJ didn't treat Hook like an equal player. Sure, he passed to him more than anyone else, but only out of necessity and usually that first pass, expecting to get it back. When he didn't, he got pissed.

"We'll never win if you split us up."

"You're not winning now, and I want to see how the two of you carry yourselves with other players. It's only for one period. I want to see lots of passing." Dax rested his hand on TJ's shoulder. "Every team is going to have great players and players who are at a lower level. It's a leader's job to raise those players up. That's what I want to see you do." Dax had no idea if this speech was going to get through to the boy or not. But it was worth a shot. If he could defy his father and do what was best for the team, he had a shot at making the team.

If he didn't, well, he could attend CFW, and even try out again as a walk-on, but he wouldn't make Dax's team on talent alone.

And Dax would be able to back up his choices.

"Okay, Coach." TJ turned and headed toward the bench.

The kid was pretty much just like his dad at that age.

Dax raced back over to the stands, ignoring the heckles from Serena asking what the hell that was all about. He sat back down next to Jim.

"That was ballsy," Jim said. "And Toby stood up and paced while his wife huffed a bunch of words I don't want to repeat."

"I'm not surprised." Dax leaned forward and rubbed his hands together. TJ came out with his new linemates.

Toby stood and turned. "Did you have something to do with this?" He pointed at Dax.

Ignore him.

"You don't know those kids or their skill level," Toby said. "This is a bad idea. It's not going to win the game. It's only going to make those boys look like they don't know what they're doing."

Serena jumped to her feet. "You're only trying to sabotage my son. If you cut TJ, I'm taking it to the board." She folded her arms and turned away.

"Those are fighting words," Jim whispered.

"She can do whatever she wants, but I want to see if TJ can be a leader or not. It will come down to how he responds to his parents' behavior. Whenever Toby was put in this situation, he ended up trying to win games on his own. Those were always his worst performances and that's why he never went anywhere." Dax swallowed his beating heart as Toby made his way to the corner of the rink.

That wasn't good.

"You know what to do," Toby shouted.

The ref dropped the puck. Tillman managed to hold it to his stick and muscle through the line. He skated wide across center ice, his right wing following a few paces behind. Tillman crossed the blue line, passing the defenseman.

His right wingman raced toward the net, completely open.

Dax shot to his feet. "Pass the puck," he whispered.

"Take it around the net to the goalie's weak side and stuff it," Toby yelled. "You got this."

"Don't do it," Dax said. "Look up and pass."

But TJ did what his father expected and the goalie covered the puck.

The next play wasn't much different, except the puck came off the goalie's stick and the other team recovered.

"Get off the ice," Toby yelled. The only reason for that was if TJ got off in time, he might not get the negative point, but it was too late. The other team scored.

Toby turned and jogged up to where Dax stood. "That goal is on you."

"I don't see how." Dax shouldn't have opened his mouth.

"I shouldn't have to tell you that every line needs to be balanced. But you can't put my son with the weakest defense line and two of the weakest wings and expect them to hold the line."

"What I expected was for TJ to pass. You can tell him that." Dax sat down and jotted a few things on his clipboard, documenting everything.

Toby muttered something under his breath as he turned and made his way to the bottom of the stands.

"I'm surprised he didn't rip you a new asshole," Jim said.

"He knows I'm right." At least Dax hoped that was the case.

Hook's line came out.

"This could be interesting," Jim said. "Hook is literally playing with the two weakest players on the team. As a matter of fact, neither one of them are going out for prep schools. They want to play regular high school and maybe club hockey when they go to college."

"Good to know," Dax said. "Interesting that Toby made a big deal about who his son was playing with."

"He's worried his kid isn't going to make any team. And he should be. But you being here is having a positive effect on his mouth."

Dax wasn't so sure about that.

Once the ref dropped the puck, Hook pushed it to his left wing, who carried it to the blue line and dumped it in. Hook chased it down behind the net and looked up.

He passed it to the right wing and cut right to the

net and took a shot, but missed. The puck came back out to the left defenseman who shot it back down behind the net where Hook picked it up again.

"Back to the blue line, kid," Dax whispered.

That's exactly what Hook did where the defenseman took a snapshot and the right wing tipped it in.

"That was a smart play," Dax said with some pride. "He certainly can read the ice. Why isn't he playing center all the time?"

"That I can't answer."

"Looks like you and I might be battling over that one," Dax said.

Jim laughed. "How long are you going to be here today?"

"Through dinner I suspect."

"Let me buy you a beer later."

"Sure." Dax narrowed his stare as he felt the metal under his feet vibrate. "Well, shit. Here comes trouble."

"You have fun with them. I'm out of here." Jim took off like a bat out of hell as Serena and Toby stomped up the bleachers.

Dax looked over them at the game, trying to ignore their angry stares.

"You had no right to mess with the lines like that," Toby said. "That's not your team. They aren't your players."

"I'm not going to have any discussion with you about hockey." Dax took his clipboard and held it to his chest. He wouldn't put it past Serena and Toby to try to find out anything and everything they could about Dax's picks for the team. "Either you can step out of my space, or I'll go watch a different game. It's up to you."

"Just tell me why you want to make my son look bad?" Serena asked with crocodile tears.

God, he hated that.

He ran a hand over the top of his head. "After the game, you can ask your son what I told him I wanted. Outside of that, we have nothing to say to one another."

TJ came out on the ice again. He glanced toward the stands.

Dax felt bad for the kid. There was nothing worse than being on the ice and seeing your parents were more interested in being engaged with someone in the stands versus the action on the ice. Dax opted to keep his attention focused on TJ, in hopes that helped the boy change his attitude.

But it didn't.

TJ did the same selfish kind of plays he'd always done.

"You're going to pay for making our son look less than the star player he is," Serena said. "I know things about you and Chablis and I'm not afraid to tell the world."

"Don't threaten me," Dax said. "You will regret it." He gathered his belongings and made his way to another rink. He couldn't imagine what bullshit rumors Serena was blubbering about and he knew there were a few. All ridiculous and he honestly didn't care what people thought. He and Chablis knew what happened between them and that's all that mattered.

7

CHABLIS

C hablis stood in front of the brewery at the edge of town and stared at the drape over the side. Axel stood next to Dax in front of it while the mayor went on about Dax's career and Axel's ability to capture it in art.

"And without further ado, I'm honored to unveil this incredible tribute to one of hockey's greatest players of all times." The mayor handed Axel a pair of scissors. "Would you like to cut the ribbon?"

"Hell, yes." Axel snipped the black and gold fabric and down came the curtain.

The crowd went nuts.

"That's amazing." Her mother took her hand and squeezed.

"I didn't expect it to be so big." Dax's face took up a quarter of the building. She'd have to look at that every time she came into town, which was every time she came home from the station.

"Or lifelike. It really looks exactly like him," his mother said. "Damn, that boy is sexy."

"Mother. Don't say stuff like that. It's weird."

"But it's true," her mom said.

"Do you have any idea how creepy it sounds when it's my ex-boyfriend?"

"Riesling gets upset when I talk about how adorable Trey's butt is."

"Gross, Mother." Chablis shook her head. "Does Dad hear you say this shit?"

"All the time." Her father came up behind her, putting his arm around her waist, startling her.

She jumped.

Her dad laughed. "She does it because it bothers you girls. If you acted like it was no big deal, she'd stop."

"That's what you say about so many things, but she never stops. Never."

Chablis looked into her father's loving eyes. "Dad. It's got to bother you."

"Nope." He kissed her temple. "You should hear the things I say to your brothers."

"That's disgusting." She folded her arms and focused on Dax who stepped up to the podium. He never liked being the center of attention, except for on the ice. "Both of you be quiet. I want to hear what Dax has to say."

"First, I want to thank Axel for this amazing work of art. I'm truly humbled," Dax said.

The crowd roared.

Axel gave a slight nod.

"I also want to thank all of you for coming out today. A special thank you to my parents for the years of driving me to early morning hockey practice and to my sisters for spending hours at the rink watching me play. And to everyone here in Candlewood Falls for supporting my career. It's truly been an amazing ride and I look forward to the next chapter as the coach of the Candlewood Falls Prep team."

Once again, the crowd went crazy.

Chablis looped her arm around her father's and leaned into his strong frame. She hung on Dax's every word. His deep voice rumbled in her belly. While he'd changed, the young man she'd fallen in love with was still at the foundation of his heart.

Dax finished his speech and all the local reporters rushed him, shoving their microphones in his face and shouting questions.

"He's going to be a while," her father said. "Want to get some ice cream?"

"I'd love some."

Her father took her mom's hand and Chablis followed her parents through the maze of townspeople.

"Oh, look." Her mother pointed. "It's Dax's parents and his two sisters. Let's join them."

It had been a while since Chablis had spent any

time with either Nova or Camila. They'd been in high school when she left town and since she and Dax ended their relationship, she avoided his family.

Hell, she avoided everyone in Candlewood Falls. She'd wanted nothing to do with anything that might remind her of Dax and of her own family.

When she'd decided to come back, she did so quietly and did her best to keep to herself. That had been in part because she had a lot of fences to mend with her own family. She had barely spoken to Malbec and Merlot over the years, unless she had to. She and Riesling were closer, but even they were strained. The twins and Zinfandel were different, but they were babies when she left. And they were raised so differently. They were like Switzerland when it came to family feuds.

"Dorothy." Weezer raised her hand and waved.

"Since when are you and Dorothy Fabion besties?" Chablis asked.

Her mother ignored her as she took a few long strides toward Dorothy and gave her a big hug. "It's so good to see you. Dax's speech was amazing."

"I can't believe that painting that Axel did on the building. I had no idea what to expect, but it wasn't that," Dorothy said.

"It's incredible." Ken, Dax's father, stretched out his arm and took Chablis' father's hand. "It's good to see you, Carter. You're looking well."

"You too," her dad said. "Hello, Nova. Camila."

"Mr. River." Nova nodded. "Chablis. We heard about what happened. We're so glad you're okay."

"You must have been so frightened," Camila added. "But we were told your actions saved so many lives."

"It's my job." Chablis felt her cheeks heat. She'd been in this situation before and it always made her squirm in her skin. She didn't like feeling as though what she did was special. Or that she held some kind of superpower. She'd been trained to fight fires. To be a first responder. It was a job. And she performed her duties well.

"And it's a hard one," Ken said. "Thank you for your service."

"You're welcome," she said.

"Shall we go get a round of ice cream for everyone?" her father asked.

"I was just about to go get in line," Ken said.

Everyone shouted out their orders and Ken and her dad left the ladies at the table. It had been a long time since these two families sat together around a table. The last time might have been when Dax was nineteen and his last year playing juniors in Canada. While her mom and Dorothy didn't see eye to eye on most things, they put down their differences whenever the families were together, even if they didn't believe Chablis and Dax should be together and both vocalized that thought.

Weezer did so more strongly, but his family wanted

him to chase his dream just as much as her family wanted her to be part of the business.

"How are you feeling?" Dorothy asked. "Do the burns still really hurt?"

"They look worse than they feel," Chablis said. "I'm super glad my headache is basically gone. That was the worst."

"It was scary to see that explosion on television and know you were right there." Dorothy leaned across the table and patted Chablis' hand.

Chablis leaned back in her chair and soaked in the spring sun as it beat down on her face.

Dax was wrapping up with the press. Poor guy. She knew how much he hated that kind of attention. She remembered the first time he'd been interviewed by the local sportscaster after his freshman debut on the CFW Prep team. When they watched it together, he'd turned six different shades of red. He'd buried his face in his hands and told her he never wanted to watch himself again.

"Looks like Dax is almost done," Camila said.

"You all must be so glad to have him back in Candlewood Falls," Chablis' mother said.

"We certainly are." Dorothy smiled wide. Her cheeks plumped out.

"I have to say I was worried that coaching a high school team wouldn't be enough for him," Nova said. "But he seems to be thriving with the idea."

Chablis swallowed her words. She'd thought the

same thing and wanted to ask his family if this had been his go-to-shit plan.

Because when he'd been working toward the NHL, he had a plan B if it didn't work and that was to teach and be a coach for a division one college.

So why wasn't he doing that now?

He couldn't have come back for CFW Prep and her. That didn't make sense.

Butterflies filled her stomach as he sauntered through the crowd in their direction. A few people stopped him for a picture and an autograph.

"Hello, everyone." He greeted his mom with a hug and a kiss on the cheek. Followed by his sisters, then Chablis' mom.

When he got to Chablis, there was an awkward pause before he dared to give her a brief kiss on the lips.

He pulled up a chair next to Chablis and all eyes were on the two of them.

She could feel the heat rise from her toes to her cheeks.

"That was a nice speech." Dorothy patted his knee. "And that mural. I can't get over it."

"Neither can I," Dax said. "While he did an amazing job, it's going to be a little embarrassing to drive by that all the time." Under the table, he grabbed her hand and laced his fingers between hers, resting them on his knee.

For a split second she thought about pulling away,

but it reminded her of all the times they'd done this when they'd been kids. Besides, she had agreed to date him.

Hand-holding went along with that.

"Here comes your dad with ice cream," Dorothy said. "We can send him back in with your order."

"I'll just share with Chablis." Dax winked.

"Lucky for you I ordered a dish; otherwise, you'd be shit out of luck." Her father set a large Sunday with all the toppings in front of her. Dax quickly got up and snagged another spoon.

"So, what is everyone planning on doing now that the parade is over?" Nova asked.

"Chablis and I are going to grab dinner and maybe catch a movie." Dax held her gaze and smiled. "Alone, so don't get any ideas about tagging along for old times' sake."

"Sounds like a hot date," Camila teased.

"I wouldn't go that far," Chablis said.

Dax cocked his head and narrowed his eyes.

She wasn't ready to deal with their families getting up in their business. The fact that they were hanging out and doing things together caused enough teasing. Declaring they were dating would create the kind of family roasting she didn't need. Not at this juncture.

Serena and Toby stepped into her line of vision.

Chablis groaned. She leaned into Dax. "Don't look now, but your favorite hockey parents are on their way over."

"There are two other local parents with sons trying out and they don't constantly come up to me every time I set foot out of my house." Dax tugged at his jeans, shifting in his seat. "I've been well behaved, but I'm going to lose my cool and it's not going to be pretty."

"Don't do that, son." His father had always been a soft-spoken man. He rarely yelled during a hockey game, usually sitting by himself in the stands, ignoring the rest of the crazies. He often had to endure other parents calling his son arrogant, selfish, and so full of himself that eventually it was going to catch up to him and no one was going to want to coach him.

None of that was true.

Dax didn't get special treatment.

But Dax was special and everyone knew it.

"Losing your temper is only going to cost you a bit of your reputation and when it comes to Toby, we both know that doesn't end well," his father said. "Bite your tongue and keep your cool."

"Easier said than done, Dad." Dax let out a short breath.

"She's still a mean girl," Nova said. She lifted her water bottle to her lips and chugged. "I didn't really know her when we were kids, but I heard stories. And as an adult, it appears she hasn't changed. She came up to me today and started telling me how great her son is and how I should tell my brother that."

"She's a piece of work, that one." Chablis couldn't

agree more. She could understand wanting the best for your kid and she certainly knew what it was like to have a meddling parent.

She could almost relate to Serena's son, TJ, on one level. It wasn't easy growing up as Weezer's daughter because Weezer had her hand in everything.

And that wasn't an exaggeration.

About the only thing that her mother let her do was make a few poor choices about drinking. Weezer's philosophy on that was to learn the hard way. Get good and drunk once and you probably won't ever want to do it again.

It worked for all Weezer's kids.

The other thing that her mom did for her kids was teach them all that life wasn't easy. It was fucking hard. And it wasn't fair and it could be cruel, especially when you least expected it.

Chablis couldn't fault her mother for some of the things she'd done, considering what had been done to her, but that didn't excuse the lies and manipulations.

Granted, her mom had turned over a new leaf and was doing her best to be a new and improved Weezer. A softer and gentler version of her harsh self. And she'd been doing a damn good job. But she was still the Weezer.

"She's not going to like when I show up at the rink this week," Chablis said.

Nova leaned forward, resting her hands on the

table. "I would like to be a fly on the wall when she finds out."

"Don't say anything. They might go tell the board and cause a stink," Dax whispered as Serena and Toby were only about twenty paces away. "I was hoping they were coming in this direction to bother someone else, but that was wishful thinking." Dax grabbed her hand. This time he didn't do it under the table and she figured it was more for moral support than a romantic gesture because he squeezed it so hard she checked to make sure her fingers weren't turning white.

"Hello, everyone," Serena said with a bright smile as if she weren't a bitch. "What a lovely parade."

"It was nice," Weezer said.

"I'm so proud of my son." Dorothy patted Dax's shoulder. "I'm glad the town came together to honor his accomplishments."

Toby glanced at his watch. "We need to get to the rink. Shouldn't you be headed there as well?" He stared at Dax with a narrowed stare.

"I'm not going today. I'll be there tomorrow." Dax leaned back and folded his arms.

The tension between the two men was palpable.

Chablis remembered all the times in high school when Toby and Dax would get into it. Toby usually started it, and most of the time he finished it, but every once in a while, Dax would lose his cool. Never with his fists. Not off the ice. But he had a nasty side to him when he was backed into a corner.

"Don't you think that's irresponsible of you?" Serena said. "You've got a team to pick. Not to mention a bunch of young teenage boys who will be disappointed and concerned they don't stand a chance if you're not there. You're sending the wrong message."

"Serena, that's enough," Toby said.

"Everyone knew I wouldn't be there," Dax said in a calm and rational tone. "I told each child that has expressed an interest in CFW Prep that I wouldn't be in attendance today, and why. So, it's not a problem." Dax dropped his hands to his lap and leaned forward. The corner of his mouth tipped upward. "I'm surprised that TJ didn't inform you of this."

"Not the point," Serena said in a huff. "We need to speak with you privately."

"About what?" Dax said with a long breath.

"Our son." Serena cocked his head. "It will only take a moment of your time."

"Serena, this isn't the time," Toby said.

Chablis was shocked that Toby was going against his wife and trying to give Dax any breathing room at all. But perhaps they were playing good cop-bad cop.

"Serena. I've told you before. We can't have any conversations until after the team is picked." Dax rubbed the back of his neck. He did that when his frustration was about to get the better of him.

Chablis squeezed his thigh.

He took her hand.

"You're not being fair to our kid because of your

problems with Toby," Serena said. "It's obvious you're letting your past jealousy of my husband—"

"That's the most absurd thing I've ever heard." Dax pushed himself to a standing position.

"Is it?" Serena planted a hand on her hip. "You had the coach switch his line to make him look bad all because you've never liked my husband."

"I switched that line because I wanted to see if TJ would step up and be a leader." Dax tapped his knuckles a little too harshly on the table. "Because we have a history, I'll break my rule about giving parents advice, but you're not going to like what I have to say."

Chablis braced herself for what could be an all-out brawl as Dax leaned a little closer to Toby.

"TJ has more talent than you did, but he can't read the ice, and do you know why that is? I'll tell you," Dax said. "It's because he has singular focus and that's to score. The game of hockey is about playing as a team to win. Not as an individual to score. Get that concept out of his head and help him understand he's not the only one on the ice and he might stand a chance. But if he keeps playing like you did, he's not going to make any prep school team this year."

"Are you threatening to sabotage our son?" Serena asked with a screech.

"That's not what I said." Dax shook his head.

"Sure sounds like it to me," Serena said. "And if our boy doesn't make a team, we'll know it's because of you." Serena looped her arm through Toby's. "If that happens, we'll have to tell everyone what we know about what Chablis did."

"Serena," Toby said with a tight jaw. "Stop that."

"What the hell does that mean?" Dax slammed his hand against the table. It rattled, sending a spoon to the ground. "Now who is threatening whom?"

"We need to go, dear." Serena and Toby turned and scurried off into the crowd.

Chablis held her breath. She placed a hand over her stomach that flipped.

Then flopped.

Then churned.

She swallowed the sour taste that filled her mouth.

There was no way Serena could know about the abortion. She had to be referencing something else. But what? Chablis had been a good girl growing up. Not a Goody Two-shoes since she'd done her fair share of rebelling, like every teenager. However, for the most part she'd been a rule follower. If her mother told her to be home by ten, she was home by ten fifteen. She never once snuck out of the house. She did, however, sneak out of her room or snuck Dax into it.

"I can't believe I fucking fell into that trap," Dax muttered as he dropped back into his seat. "I wonder what kind of bullshit lie they will make up to try to hurt you if no one takes TJ."

"Don't you worry about me," Chablis said with as strong a voice as she could muster. "They probably don't have anything and are now scrambling to find a blemish on my firefighting record, or maybe something wicked I did in high school or college."

"Worse thing you ever did was thinking you got away with stealing kisses with Dax out in the vineyard after you thought we all went to bed," her mother teased. "Only I had spies and if I thought things were getting too hot and—"

"Mother." Chablis' cheeks heated. "That's enough."

"So many things make sense now." Dax laughed. He took her by the arm and helped her to her feet. "If you all don't mind, Chablis and I are going to walk around town."

"Go. Enjoy yourselves," her mother said.

Her father hugged her.

His sisters and parents gave a big wave.

Chablis held on to Dax's biceps as they strolled away from their families and into the crowd of people. Her stomach had yet to calm from the unsettling conversation with Serena and Toby.

The only thing in Chablis' past that could come back and hurt Dax would be the fact she never told him about the abortion.

That had to be what they were talking about, and she had to tell him before they did.

8

DAX

Dax's heart hammered in the back of his throat. He wanted everything to be perfect. He'd gone to great lengths to pull this off and it had to look just like it had on the night he'd told her that he loved her and that they'd made love for the first time.

They had been young. Perhaps too young.

But they'd been in love and at the time, he didn't think he'd ever want anyone but Chablis.

Nearly two decades later, that statement was true. He might have had other women and short-lived affairs, but he'd never loved anyone other than Chablis.

He tugged her toward the back parking lot of her family winery where'd he secured the use of the ATV from Malbec, who'd given him permission to set up a little romantic table setting out by the river's edge at the furthest point of the property. No one ever went back there, which is why Chablis and Dax used to go there as teenagers.

"What are you doing?" Chablis paused when Dax climbed onto the ATF.

"We're going for a ride."

"Why and where?"

"A trip down memory lane," he said. "Now get on."

Chablis took a step back. Her gaze shifted between him and the back of the vehicle.

He loved the way her nose crinkled.

"The last time we went out there, it wasn't to talk," she said softly.

He chuckled, taking her hand as she lifted her leg, climbing on behind him and wrapping her arms around his body. "Perhaps I'm not in the mood to talk now," he said. "Do you remember how long it took to walk out to the river's edge?"

"I walk it on a regular basis. I have to get my steps in somehow. Besides, I'm wearing a skirt."

"That doesn't bother me. Now, I'm an impatient man, so let's get going." He turned the key to the ATV and revved the engine. "Hang on." He hit the gas and the machine lurched forward.

She grabbed his waist. Tight.

He'd missed her arms around his body. It reminded him of the final pieces of a puzzle and how it felt to sit back and look at the masterpiece that had taken so long to put together. The overwhelming sense of satisfaction of completing something beautiful.

He wanted that sensation for life and Chablis was the only person who could give it to him. Without her, he was simply a man who played professional hockey at one time. Sure, he was one of the best. He'd won a few Stanley Cups. He'd eventually be inducted into the Hockey Hall of Fame. He knew many players wanted what he had and he was grateful and proud of his accomplishments.

But that choice came at a cost.

A big one.

He'd lost the love of his life.

And now he had to earn her love back.

He took the trail that led toward the cottage where her little sister Zinfandel lived. He'd been told by Malbec that Zinfandel was headed out of town for the night, so she wouldn't be around.

After he passed the cottage, he looped to the smaller trail that followed the property line between the winery and the alpaca farm until they got to the bend in the river. He parked the ATV near the footpath and help Chablis off the vehicle. His pulse pushed against his skin. He hadn't felt this nervous since he'd been called up from the farm team.

She was being unusually quiet, even for her, considering she wasn't known for small talk. If there wasn't anything to say, Chablis didn't fill the air with useless words. She was one of the few people he knew who could be comfortable with silence.

He admired that about her.

He lifted a picnic basket off the ATV, laced his fingers through hers, and tugged her toward the small clearing where they used to go when they were kids. It was off the beaten path and no one would see them unless they came looking.

And no one would.

He'd come to this spot before the parade and made sure everything had been set up. Unfortunately, he had to do some clearing of bushes since no one had been there in years. Hopefully, she'd appreciate his efforts.

"I haven't been back here since you left," she whispered. "I'm surprised it's... Oh, my God." She covered her mouth as they stepped into the clearing. "What the hell have you done?"

In the center of the small area he'd set up a blanket which had been held down by some rocks on the corners. In the center was a bouquet of red and pink roses.

It was exactly as it was the first time they'd made love.

He set the basket down and took her in his arms, staring deep into her kind, loving eyes. He could get lost in those pools of deep desire. "I know we can't go back, but I wanted to remind both of us of what we once meant to each other."

Her mouth tipped into a smile. "Neither one of us are living at home. We can have sex either at your place or mine."

"That's not the only reason I wanted to come out here," he said. "Do you remember our first time?"

She dropped her head to his chest. "I had no idea what I was doing."

"Oh. And I did?" He chuckled. He remembered it like it was yesterday. He'd been home for a long weekend and they'd been talking about the possibility of taking things to the next level. Everyone thought they had broken up and they wanted their families to believe that.

He'd been tired of his family telling him she was a distraction and she'd been tired of her family telling her that they could never make it work. She was staying in Candlewood Falls and he would be chasing a dream.

"Serena and her friends put it in my head that you had to be doing it with other girls behind my back."

Dax lifted her chin with his thumb and forefinger. He remembered all the rumors people had started about him, especially Serena and Toby. "I only had eyes for you."

"I knew that, but it was hard with you being gone so much, knowing that you were probably going to make it to the NHL and I was going to follow in my mother's footsteps. That made our relationship doomed from the beginning and I think we both knew it."

"It doesn't make what we had any less special." Staring into the depths of her soul, he fell in love with her all over again. A warmth spread across his skin like water beads from a shower coating his body. "The only regret I have when it comes to you is that we hurt each other." He palmed her cheek. "I'm sorry I was so cruel when I told you to go home."

A single tear rolled down her cheek.

He kissed it away.

"I did the same thing to you more than once." She leaned into him, wrapping her arms around his shoulders. "I didn't want you to give up your dreams for me. That wouldn't have been right. You worked too hard not to chase it and if you hadn't, you would have resented me."

"You're right about that," he admitted the truth, even though it left a horrible taste in his mouth. He'd accepted the fact that they needed to go their separate ways, but now it was time to come back together and he wanted to do it by starting over where they'd shared their most vulnerable moments.

Their deepest secrets and fears.

This had been their spot and he needed to not only rekindle their passion, but their trust.

"We can both agree that we did what we thought we needed to at the time. However, I've missed you." He brushed his lips over her mouth. He only wanted a brief taste, but he quickly deepened the kiss. Holding her tight against his chest, he couldn't let go. He'd become desperate. He slipped his hands under her shirt, needing to feel her bare skin under his fingertips.

He'd been with other women, but it all came back to one.

To Chablis.

His first love.

His only love.

He helped her to the blanket while keeping their lips entangled in a wild kiss. He rolled to his back, enjoying her full weight on the length of his body. He found her bra strap and fiddled with the hook.

Only it didn't come undone quickly.

She pressed her hand against his chest and stiffened her spine. "There's something we need to talk about."

"Now?" He blinked. "Can't it wait?"

She tucked her long hair behind her ears. "It's about Serena and the dirt she thinks she has on me."

Dax rolled his eyes and groaned. "That woman is the last person I want to talk about while you're lying on top of me like this." He squeezed her ass. "Besides, whatever she thinks she has doesn't matter. She's full of crap and she'll make up anything."

"I have a few skeletons," Chablis whispered. "And there's one you need to know."

He pressed his finger over her lips. "Whatever it is, I'm sure it's not as bad as you believe it is." He leaned forward and kissed her, hard. He wanted her to feel how much he desired her in the moment. The past didn't matter. Only this moment did. "I care about you so much."

"I care about you too," she whispered.

"I want you. Right here. Right now. We can talk later."

"You brought me out here to seduce me?"

"Something like that." He turned his gaze to the basket, which had been knocked over along with the flowers." There's a bottle of wine and some cheese and crackers. We can slow down if you want, but yeah. That was kind of the point."

"What is it about you and being naked in broad daylight outside?"

She reached behind her back and unfastened the article of clothing before slipping it through the sleeve of her shirt and tossing it aside.

He swallowed. She was still completely covered.

But her breasts pushed against the thin fabric, leaving nothing to the imagination.

"It's dusk and soon it will be dark."

"Doesn't answer my question." She toyed with the hem of her shirt.

He wiggled his feet, kicking off his shoes. "It's not a fascination because I've only had sex outside with you."

"I find that hard to believe." She lifted her shirt and threw that to the ground.

Her hair tumbled back down over her torso.

He brushed it over her shoulders, staring seamlessly at her nakedness. She had to be the most beautiful creature he'd ever had the pleasure of laying eyes on and he didn't want to stop gawking. He traced a path with his index finger from her belly button to under her breast. "It's true," he said softly, keeping his focus on the way her body responded to his touch.

They weren't teenagers learning about sex anymore. They were grown adults who'd had other partners. It wasn't even like they'd had a lot of sex. Maybe ten times total, so he wasn't entirely sure what she liked or didn't like. For the first time in a long while, he was nervous about pleasing a woman.

But only because this no ordinary lady.

Chablis was special.

She was the one.

And he had to prove he was worthy.

He sat up, bringing his lips to her nipple. It puckered under his kiss.

She arched into him, gripping his shoulders and moaning softly. Before he could protest, she was undoing his pants, lowering his zipper, and taking him into her soft mouth.

He pooled her hair onto the top of her head and enjoyed the view, as well as the sensations, though it wouldn't last very long. Even the first time she'd done this, she'd mastered it. Of course, there was nothing like having someone you loved please you and all he wanted to do was make her happy.

"Hey. Up here." He tugged gently.

She kissed her way up his chest.

"You're so beautiful," he whispered, rolling her to her back. He ran his hand up her bare leg and under her skirt. He palmed her before slipping two fingers inside. He lifted them to his lips and tasted. "Mmmm-mmm." Everything about Chablis excited Dax.

The way she squirmed and wiggled under his kisses gave him great satisfaction. He loved the way her fingers dug into his shoulders as he settled between her legs. Or the way she whispered his name while her hips rolled against his mouth.

Or how her muscles tensed and her breathing became more labored.

She clutched his head, squeezing her thighs. Her body quivered. "Dax," she said in a throaty moan. "Yes."

He found her mouth and kissed her hard. He thrust inside her, hoping it wasn't too aggressive.

By the way her hips were grinding against him, he decided it was exactly the way she wanted. And she didn't let up. She wrapped her feet around the back of this thighs, locking her ankles.

Even when they'd been young and inexperienced, they'd been able to set off fireworks.

This evening was no exception.

Her second orgasm rocked them both, forcing his climax to the surface.

"Chablis," he whispered in her ear, kissing her neck. He could only hope he'd be enough for her. That she'd find her way back to loving him.

He ran his hands up and down her back, letting his fingers get tangled up in her long, thick hair. He let it cascade over her glistening skin. Taking in a deep breath, he let it out slowly. He blinked his eyes a few times, staring at the darkening sky as the sun set behind the horizon.

She rolled to her side, curling up next to him, draping her leg and arm over him while he pulled part of the blanket across their naked bodies. Stars began to appear. He loved this time of night. And he loved being back in this spot with Chablis.

"This has always been my favorite place in Candlewood Falls," he said.

"Why? Because it's where you lost your virginity?"

"No. Because it's where I fell in love with you."

"I'm naked. You don't need to flatter me to get me out of my pants." She propped her chin on his chest. "Besides, I thought we were going to put that kind of talk on the back burner and just date."

He chuckled. "That kind of went out the window about fifteen minutes ago."

She reached across him and found her shirt. Quickly, she dressed herself and sat cross-legged. "I'm sorry, but us sleeping together doesn't change the fact I'm not ready to move past dating."

He found his pants and wiggled back into them. He ran a hand across the top of his head, slightly confused. Because he wanted her so badly, he'd jump through whatever hoops she wanted. However, he needed to understand what and why. "What you're saying is that you don't feel as strongly for me as I do for you."

"I'm saying that there are things in my past that you

don't know about." Chablis grabbed a large portion of her hair and twisted. "I did something and I really have no idea how to tell you." She sniffled.

"Hey." He took her chin with his thumb and forefinger. "A lot has happened to both of us over the last seventeen years. My past isn't all that rosy either. I've been in a couple barroom brawls. Two of which ended up with me checking out the inside of county lockup."

"I heard about those." She turned her head and swiped at her cheeks. "This isn't the same."

The sound of something vibrating caught his attention, but he did his best to ignore it. "Whatever it is, I'm sure it's not as bad as you think it is."

"Where's my purse? That's my phone."

"It can wait." He cupped her cheeks.

The vibration paused for only a few seconds before starting again.

"Talk to me," he said.

"Someone is trying to reach me." She found her bag and dug her hand into it, pulling out her cell. "It's my mom. She's called three times. She never does that unless it's important."

Dax let out a long breath and leaned back.

"Mom? What's going on?" Chablis held the phone to her ear. Her eyes grew wide and she gasped, covering her mouth. "Oh no. When?"

Dax scooted closer, sensing something terrible had happened.

"Okay. I'll be there as soon as I can."

"What's wrong?" Dax put a protective arm around Chablis.

"It's my father. He collapsed and hit his head. He might have had a heart attack. He's in the ambulance now on the way to the hospital. I have to go."

Dax was on his feet. "Come on. I'll drive you."

"That's not necessary."

"Perhaps not. But I'm going to anyway." No way would he let her sit there by herself. This is one of the ways he could show her how much he cared and that whatever skeleton she had, they'd deal with it.

9

CHABLIS

Even though Chablis' father had been discharged from the hospital with a mild concussion after fainting because he'd been dehydrated and been in the sun too long—not heart problems, thank goodness—Chablis had still spent the night tossing and turning.

Not to mention her burns continued to throb. However, they were healing nicely and her headaches were totally gone at this point.

Dax had dropped her off around midnight. He'd kissed her good night like he had every intention of sleeping. She nearly caved, but things with him were moving too fast.

And they still needed to talk, but her emotions were running too hot last night, so she'd tabled the conversation for another day and Dax respected her wishes and went home.

He'd texted her before he left for the rink and left a single rose on her doorstep with a sweet note.

With no job to scurry off to and no Sunday family dinner to attend, Chablis decided to do exactly what everyone told her not to do.

Head to the rink.

But not before getting a tall mug of fresh coffee and a big fat chocolate croissant from the Green Bean.

She found a spot on the street to park and strolled to the sidewalk where the line was out the door. It always was on a Sunday. She checked her cell. No messages from anyone. She should consider that a good thing, but her stomach had been in a tight knot ever since Serena had approached them yesterday and it had gotten worse after she and Dax had made love.

She shouldn't have let it go that far with him before telling him what she'd done. Deep down she knew she'd made the right decision.

For both of them.

Even if he had agreed with her choice and held her hand through the process, it would have split his focus during that first important month of his career. It would have changed the trajectory and he still would have resented her for it.

However, that didn't change the fact that in the present, if they were going to make a second go of it, he needed to know and it had to come from her. No one else. The only question was, how on earth was she going to tell him?

"Well, if it isn't Chablis River," a woman with a slightly Southern accent said.

Alison Weatherby.

Wonderful.

Chablis turned and smiled. "Good morning, Mrs. Weatherby."

"Why, it's five minutes after noon," Mrs. Weatherby said, blinking her fake eyelashes. Her big old dark hair was piled high on top of her head. The woman looked like she walked right out of a nineteen-fifties magazine, white gloves and all. "How is your father? We heard he took a tumble right on the sidewalk. Your poor mama. She must have been so scared. Though, I can't imagine the Weezer frightened of anything."

"Thank you for asking," Chablis said, doing her best to keep a kind tone. "My dad is just fine."

"Well, thank goodness for small favors."

The best favor of all would be for this damn line to get moving faster.

"I'm also glad that you're looking relatively well."

Relatively? What the hell did that mean? Alison Weatherby didn't know how to hand out a compliment without making an insult first.

"Though, firefighting business should be left to the men." She let out a long breath. "I'm just not a fan of all that women's lib stuff."

Chablis wasn't going to touch that one with a ten-foot pole. She decided to keep her mouth shut. She didn't have anything nice to say, so she might as well say nothing.

A few moments of silence ticked by as the line moved about three people into the store. But there were a good ten customers in front of her.

"My daughter tells me she keeps seeing you and Dax around town. Are the two of you an item?" Alison asked.

"We're friends," Chablis said. She wasn't prepared to tell the world they were dating because she wasn't exactly sure that was what they were doing. It wasn't a well-defined relationship. Not yet anyway.

"It's probably a good thing that you're not together." Alison tilted her head, giving it a little nod as if she felt sorry for Chablis for some reason. "Considering he's probably not going to stay in Candlewood Falls very long."

"Excuse me?"

"Oh. I guess you don't know."

"Know what?"

"I heard through some friends of mine that he's applied to coach a division one college in Massachusetts." Alison made a *tsk* noise with her mouth. "I think he should step down immediately so they can find a replacement."

While Chablis' heart tumbled to her gut like a ship sinking to the bottom of the ocean, she tried not to act like she was completely blindsided. Colleges were finishing up their season and most had already made their announcements of staffing changes. If this were true, Dax would already be heading out the door. Unless this was for a future position next year.

Her blood turned hot.

How could she think a man as talented as Dax would ever be satisfied coaching teenagers?

"Gossiping is a good look for you, Mrs. Weatherby." Chablis felt the need to use Alison's proper name, though not out of respect. "If you will excuse me, I forgot something in my car."

"Would you like me to hold your spot, dear?"

"No, thank you," Chablis mumbled. She decided the coffee at the rink would be good enough, if she stayed long enough to get one.

That all depended on Dax's answer to her question.

Dax

Dax had no idea how his coaches managed to survive picking a team. It wasn't just dealing with the crazy parents, but rifling through the talent.

And there were some really great hockey players to pick from.

He stretched out his legs and leaned against the back of the cold stands.

"Hey, Dax," Jim said. "How's it going today?"

"Not bad. You?"

"This is my last game, and then I'm headed back home. I'll be back down for the all-stars game to look at a couple of other boys, but for the most part, I'm pretty locked in these six boys." Jim flipped his clipboard over and showed off a list of names. Two of which were young men that Dax was interested in as well. The others hadn't even applied to his school.

"Those are fine choices."

"What about you?"

"I won't be making any decisions until the end of next week." He had crossed of at least ten boys that didn't have the drive or work ethic, much less the talent. They had the grades to get in, but that was about it. There were two no-brainers to take on the team; the rest was fair play.

Including TJ Tillman.

Heartburn filled Dax's chest. He pounded the center of it with his fist. Taking him would mean dealing with Toby and Serena on a regular basis.

But that shouldn't be the reason he didn't take the boy.

Far from it.

"I'm surprised to see you sitting at this game. Are you really considering TJ?"

"I have to," Dax said. "He's a good player."

"He's a hothead."

"I'm not going to argue that point, but I've played with kids like him, namely his father. Coached right, and without his father's influence, I bet he'd be a completely different player."

"Are you going to tell me your father didn't influence your play?" Jim cocked his head.

"Oh. He absolutely did. But my dad had a much different approach. Besides believing almost all hockey parents were assholes, he believed those with inflated or even justified egos were bound to fail."

"Your father's a smart man."

"Again, I won't argue with you." Dax had always admired his father's quiet resolve. "Stick around. I'm going to do something crazy in the third period of this game."

"What? Dare I ask."

"TJ's coach has agreed to let me run the bench any way I see fit."

The buzzer went off and the Zamboni came on the ice.

"If this kid will take direction from me with his father going ballistic in the corner, he might change the course of his hockey career." Dax jumped to his feet and jogged down the bleachers. He raced right on past Serena and Toby, who thankfully said nothing.

His heartbeat kicked up a notch. He worried that coaching wouldn't give him the same thrill, and it didn't.

But the excitement had built into the kind of frenzy he craved. The idea that he'd be standing behind these boys made his adrenaline go into high gear.

He tapped on the locker room door. "Hey, Coach," he said.

"Welcome, Coach Fabion."

Dax swallowed as the locker room went deadpan silent. The team had removed their helmets and all eyes were on him.

"Boys," the other coach began, "Coach Fabion is going take over for the rest of the game. I'm sure you don't need a lecture on respect." He turned and waved his hand in front of Dax. "The floor is yours, Coach."

"First. Please call me Coach Dax. Second. I am going to make a few quick lineup changes. TJ, you're with Boone and Jamie. Hook, I want you to center Ken and Cameron. Gerry, you've got Frank and Wes. Defense stays the same. I'm going to be making some other adjustments as I see fit. I want quick changes. I don't want anyone on the ice for more than forty-five seconds. I see a lot of good stuff going on out there, but I've spoken to a few of you individually and I want you to incorporate those changes. Now, I know most of you aren't trying out for my team. But the other coaches are out there, especially now that they've heard I'm taking over the bench. They are out there not to just to see what you can do, but what I'm going to do. So, let's show them what we've got. Okay?"

Everyone but TJ got on their feet and gave a big-ass cheer.

Dax opened the door and let the boys out. Everyone except TJ. "I need a word with you."

TJ turned in the hallway and rested his arm over his stick. "Yes, Coach?"

"I take it you have a problem with the lines."

"Not really. It's your call. But my father's not going to like it. Nor are some of the other parents."

"Why not?"

TJ glanced over his shoulder.

"This is a safe space. You can tell me."

"My parents don't like you."

"I know that," Dax said. He found it interesting that TJ focused on both his parents and not his dad. "Your folks aren't trying out for my team. You are. I'm not concerned with what the parents think of my line changes. I am, however, interested in your thoughts and why you aren't as enthusiastic as the rest of your teammates."

"Hook and I have been playing on the same line for two years. Same team since we were mites. Our parents are best friends. They want us together and I always know where he's going to be. He's the only one on this team that can skate with me."

"That's not true and I think you know that." Dax placed a hand on TJ's shoulder. "You are one of the better puck handlers, but you have a lot to learn about being a team player. I want to help make you the best hockey player you can be. But you have to be willing to work with me, not against me, and that means I can't have you listening to what your father is shouting at you from the stands. I know he means well. He's your dad and he loves you. But for the next fifteen minutes, I'm your coach and we're down by two goals. I want to win. Do you want to win?"

"Yes, Coach."

"All right. Let's go get the job done." Dax had no idea if that little pep talk got through to TJ or not, but he was about to find out. He took his spot on the bench, behind the team. He leaned over and took TJ by the helmet. "Win the puck, dump it across the blue line, and set someone up. I don't care who it is, but I want to see you pass the puck and get an assist. Not a goal. Be a leader. Got that?"

"What if I see a shot?"

"Unless you hear me yelling to take it, I want you passing."

TJ nodded. He adjusted his helmet and jumped out onto the ice.

Dax held his breath until the puck dropped. He could hear Toby yelling from the corner of the ice. So far, TJ ignored his father's wishes and did exactly what Dax had instructed him to do. He'd been on the ice for twenty-three seconds and he'd made three passes.

That's more than Dax had seen him do since he'd met the boy.

"That's it," Dax said. "Back to the point."

TJ sent it to his defenseman who wound up for the snapshot.

"Get in front of the net, TJ."

The defenseman hit the puck. It went sailing in the

air, hit the goalie's pad, and bounced out, but TJ was there and he stuffed it in for the goal.

"Yes." Dax smacked his hands together, then waved the boys off.

"What the hell are you doing taking them off the ice when they are hot? Keep my kid on," Toby yelled.

"Yeah. Put him and Hook on," another dad said.

Dax glanced up.

"That's Greg Hook," the assistant coach said.

"You did good. Real good." He smacked TJ's helmet.

"No offense, Coach, but that's with this defense. I trust them to hold the blue line. If it were with—"

"Don't even say it," Dax said with a stern voice. "If I ever hear you cutting down another teammate again, it will cost two shifts. Got it?"

"Yes, Coach." TJ shifted his gaze to his skates.

"Let's switch the defensive lines." Nothing pissed Dax off more than making another kid feel bad because he might be the weakest link on the team.

Everyone had one.

Not everyone could be the star. Dax had been blessed—or cursed—depending on how you looked at it, but he couldn't tolerate shaming another human for any reason.

While the next line was out on the ice, he got in TJ's face. "I expect you to do the same thing the next shift. We'll make adjustments as the game changes, but you listen to my voice. Not those coming from the stands."

"Yes, sir."

Someone pounding on the glass caught Dax's attention. It was Greg, and he was yelling at his kid—to, oddly, pass the puck.

Dax watched as Hook circled around the back of the net and looked up. He found a lane and passed. Three shots went off, but no goal.

The next ten minutes were scoreless, but the team played well. There were a few hiccups and Dax began to understand why TJ didn't trust the weaker defensive line, so he made a couple more adjustments, swapping a weaker player for a stronger one on each line.

It upset the parents, and even one of the coaches, but with one minute left in the game, the score was tied.

He called a time-out.

"All right, boys. Do we want to play to win or play it safe?" he asked.

"Play to win," they all shouted.

"It means for the next sixty seconds, five boys will be on the ice with maybe one or two minor changes. It means I will say who I think has played the best in this last period. I'm not saying I think these are the best players, just who played the best right now. Everyone good with that?"

"Yes," the boys yelled.

"You might not be playing *your* position. But trust that I know what I'm doing."

"You did win a few Stanley Cups," the assistant coach said. "I think we're in good hands."

Dax laughed. "Okay. I want Hook at center with Boone and Jamie." He shifted his gaze to TJ. "TJ. I need you on point with Karl. Can you do that for me?"

He nodded with wide eyes. "I know you normally play that spot on a power play, and that's how we're going to play this last minute. Like they are down a man."

"But they aren't," TJ said.

"They will be once we drop it in their zone because I will be pulling the goalie, and Ken, you'll be jumping the boards. If the puck comes out, you'll have to haul ass off the ice so the goalie can get back on. Got it?"

"That's a tricky move for a win," the assistant coach said.

"It's either that, or we play to tie." Dax shrugged. "It's up to you."

TJ jumped to his feet. "I'm in. Let's get this done." He skated to a defensive position and his father went ballistic, banging on the plexiglass.

"What the hell? My son isn't a defenseman. He leads this team in goals. What the hell are you trying to prove, Dax?" Toby shouted.

Serena yelled at TJ to take the center position. To blatantly defy his coach. She was a hundred times worse than Toby. She went after the kids, where Toby's beef right now was with Dax.

He folded his arms and waited for the puck to drop.

Hook pushed it back to Karl who skated backward and then passed the puck over to TJ.

"Keep control of the puck," Dax said.

TJ skated up the ice, across the red line. He found a lane and passed to Boone, who crossed the blue line. Jamie sprinted toward the net and Hook went to the corner.

"Now." Dax waved to the goalie. Ken had one leg over the boards waiting until the goalie was off the ice.

"Shoot, TJ!" Toby pounded on the plexiglass.

TJ passed across to the other defenseman.

"No! You should have shot the puck," Serena yelled. "Take control of the game."

TJ glanced over his shoulder as the puck came sailing back to him and he completely missed it and it crossed the blue line, which meant everyone had to come out of the zone.

"Shit," Dax mumbled. "Shut the hell up, Toby and Serena, and leave your kid alone. He's been playing great."

TJ was the closest to the bench. He flew over the boards, giving the goalie a chance to get back on the ice; however, the puck made it all the way to the other end, causing an icing call.

"Sorry, Coach." TJ kept his gaze to his feet.

"I remember how hard it was to keep my eyes on the prize when people were yelling at me in the stands."

TJ snapped his head up.

"Look. He's your dad. I get it. You don't want to let him down. It's hard. But trust me when I say, the hardest hurdle you're ever going to have to get over growing up is becoming your own man. If you want to go to CFW Prep or any of these schools and if you want to make any kind of career out of hockey, whether that be going to college, or further, you're going to have to start making some tough decisions, and one of them is going to be figuring out that sometimes, while your dad always means well, he's not helping you right now." Dax opted to leave his mother out of the picture because he wasn't so sure about her motives.

TJ's eyes teared up. "He's going to say you're sabotaging me."

"I'm not. If you look out in those stands, every single coach that is looking at you is in those stands right now. They are seeing a whole new you. Not the player they thought you were, but the player you can be. The player I want on my team. You keep this kind of play up all next week, and they will have to fight me for you."

TJ stood up a little taller.

"Can I go back out on the ice?"

"Yes." Dax nodded.

TJ took his position at point. Stick down. Head up.

The ref dropped the puck. Hook took it and dumped it back to TJ.

Once again, Toby yelled for him to shoot. TJ wound

as if he was going to, but instead, sent it over to the other point, who passed to the center.

Dax pulled the goalie and Ken raced toward the net.

"Take the shot, TJ," Dax said.

Hook passed it back. TJ got it on his stick and fired. It hit the goalie's pad, bouncing out. Ken shot again and missed, but TJ came barreling in, while Hook took his position back at point.

TJ took the rebound and scored.

Game over.

With one second to spare.

The boys on the bench went nuts.

Dax let out a sigh of relief.

"That was awesome," The assistant slapped him on the back. "You're going to make an excellent coach."

"I wasn't sure that was going to work."

"Six out of ten times it won't, especially with a kid like TJ, but you got through to him. That's a miracle by itself. I hope it sticks." The assistant pointed toward the hallway. "His dad seems to have softened this past year, but his mom is a piece of work. Rumor has it they are having marital problems."

"That's too bad." That sucked for TJ and explained a lot. Dax mentally prepared himself to deal with Toby.

"I think we need to talk." Toby stood in Dax's way with his hands on his hips.

"The only thing I have to say right now is that TJ played one hell of a period. You should be proud," Dax said, eyeing Chablis in the stands. That warmed his heart.

"I'm always proud of my son." Toby actually smiled. His eyes brightened. "I don't want to discuss his place in the hockey world. I just think it would be a good idea for the two of us to chat."

"Okay. Let's set up a time later this week. I'll text you." All Dax wanted to do right now was go see Chablis. "If you will excuse me, I have other games and players that need my attention."

10

DAX

"Hey, you." Dax smiled as he approached Chablis in the stands. "I didn't expect to see you here today, but boy, are you a sight for sore eyes."

"We need to talk," she said with a terse tone.

"Is everything okay?" he asked. "Did something happen with your dad?"

"He's fine," she said. "Can we go outside?"

"Sure." Dax followed Chablis out to the parking lot. The bright sun hit his face. He'd forgotten how cold it was inside the rink. Back in the day, he joked his veins were made of ice because the temperature of the rinks never bothered him. Still didn't, but he had to admit, he preferred the warmth of the spring air right now. "Did you see TJ play? I couldn't believe it. He actually listened to me. He did give me a little lip, but for the most part, he ignored his father. There might be hope for that kid after all." He guided her to the picnic bench by the side of the building and sat on top of the table.

"I saw. Everyone was talking about it. You should know that Serena and Toby aren't letting you have any of the credit. They are giving it all to their kid and his great ability to play the sport. You being on the bench had nothing to do with it."

"I don't want to sound like an arrogant prick, but fuck that. I was at least half the reason. The kids were the rest. They really stepped up. Every single one of them, but especially TJ. I can see that he wants this and he's more talented than Toby. Now I have to find a way to get Toby off that boy's ass. I might actually have to take Toby out for a beer or something."

"That's a scary thought." She opted to stand with her arms folded across her chest.

"Okay. I know you and you're pissed off at me about something. So what is it?"

"Massachusetts." She glared.

"What about the state?" He swallowed. He didn't have to ask what had gotten her all hot and bothered. The only questions was, how did she find out and what exactly did she think she knew?

"The division one college that you applied to coach at. That's what."

"I applied to three colleges." He held up three fingers and wiggled them. "And five prep schools. I interviewed at one college and two high schools. I took the coaching position at CWF. It was always my first choice. I made that clear to the administrators when I interviewed." He wasn't lying. However, he wasn't being totally honest either. He still had a backup plan. It wasn't that he wanted to coach anywhere else. He didn't. Not really. But there was no way he could live in Candlewood Falls forever if Chablis was going to reject him, and the jury was still out on how she felt about him.

Shit.

He should trust that she was still in love with him or why would she be so unsettled by this finding? She wouldn't feel betrayed if she didn't care for him and want him to stay. This was all about their inability to commit.

Double shit.

He could be in a committed relationship with Chablis. He could give her his heart. That was the easy part.

His problem is he didn't trust she could and maybe that right there was the biggest issue of all.

"So, you don't have an interview with a division one college in another state."

"No. I don't." He should have said *not at the moment*, but he was also going to go into his email and tell them he wasn't interested anymore. That he found a job and he was happy right where he was. He needed to take a leap of faith if he and Chablis stood a chance. If he had one foot halfway out the door, she'd sense it, and then how could he expect her to give herself completely? "I want to be here. With you."

She dropped her arms to her sides and tilted her head toward the sky. "I ran into Alison Weatherby at the Green Bean. She told me about this interview. Something about knowing people at the college."

"I'm guessing that family wouldn't mind me gone and you know she's a gossip." Dax pushed himself from the table and took Chablis into his arms. "That college won't be picking a new coach until next year. My name is still on their list."

"So she wasn't lying to me." Chablis arched a brow.

"Neither am I," he said. "I don't want that job. They haven't offered it to me, nor have they given me an interview. I do have a letter of interest that I got this week that I haven't responded to." He took her chin with his thumb and forefinger. "But I plan on telling them I've taken a job and I'm withdrawing my application."

"Don't do that on my account." She took a step back.

"Why are you so mad at me? I told you I'm not taking the job. I've been honest with you, so I don't get what I've done that's upset you." He raised his hands toward the sky before slapping his palms to his thighs. "I respected your wishes last night and left you alone, even though I was worried about you because of your dad."

"He was fine and so was I," she said.

"Fair enough." He blew out a puff of air. "I care about you and I want to give us a second chance. Do you want that?"

"What I want is to know that you're not settling on a career choice for me."

"I'm not." He inched closer and palmed her cheek. "I chased my dream. I played in the fucking NHL. I have four Stanley Cups. I lived exactly what I thought I wanted, and you know what? It was all a bit empty because I didn't have you."

She curled her fingers around his wrist. "Do you regret it?"

He shook his head. "I can't say that I do," he admitted. "But there was always a piece of me that was missing. I allowed myself to be okay with that because deep down I believed it's what you wanted me to do. Maybe I was kidding myself. You tell me."

She raised up on tiptoe and kissed his cheek. "It's exactly what I wanted for you. I watched every game. Every single one. If I was on duty and had to miss it live, I made sure I recorded it and watched it later."

"Seriously?" He smiled. His heart swelled. A small part of him expected she might have caught a couple of playoff games and definitely the Stanley Cup wins. But he never expected to hear she watched all his games. "You would have had to subscribe to the NHL package."

"I did. I still have it. You made me a die-hard hockey fan." She held his hands. "I pushed you away because I didn't want you to have regrets. If you didn't chase your dream, you would have and you telling me to go home was you finally understanding that truth."

"I can agree with that," he said. "However, if I ever thought you would have been happy walking away from your life with your family and the winery, I would have taken you along for the ride. You were dedicated to the family business. To your own career. When Malbec walked away, I didn't believe for one second that would last very long."

"Truth be told, no one did. Including Malbec." Chablis released his hands and took a step back. "That brings me to the painful part of my past that we need to talk about, but I don't want to do it here. Can we talk tonight?"

"Since your family dinner was canceled, I promised my parents I'd go to their place tonight. I was hoping you'd join me. Maybe after that we can go back to my place and have that conversation."

She patted his chest. "You should spend some time alone with your folks. Why don't we plan on tomorrow night after we deal with a few youth hockey games."

"Sounds like a plan." He cupped her chin. "Want to come back in and watch another game with me?"

"I'm going to go check on my dad, if you don't mind."

"Not at all." He took her mouth in a hot, wet kiss. The kind he used to steal when he'd sneak in her room late at night, which reminded him that she was his next-door neighbor. "If you're awake when I get home tonight, can I stop by?"

"If the light is on, but text me first."

"What if I climbed in the window like old times' sake." He winked.

"You did that once," she said. "And only because Malbec was off at college and you had no excuse for being at the house at midnight."

"I spent the entire night. I thought for sure I was going to get caught when we fell asleep and didn't wake up until the sun came out."

"You and me both," she said with a giggle. "I'm not going to make any promises that I'll be up for visitors because we really do need to have this talk before we take things any further."

"If you say so." He pressed his mouth over hers and slipped his tongue between her lips. He couldn't imagine anything in her past that would prevent them from being together. Even if she had a secret husband that she hadn't divorced yet or something as crazy as that, it wouldn't stop him from loving her. They would work through whatever it was. "I've always loved the way you kiss."

"Don't you have hockey games to watch?"

He groaned. "I'd rather spend the rest of the day watching you breathe."

"You're so weird." She patted the center of his chest. "Don't look now, but here comes your favorite hockey dad with his son."

"He wants to set up a time to chat."

"Are you going to?"

"I think it would be a good idea," Dax said. "I'm just glad that his wife isn't with him right now."

She gave him a quick kiss. "Later, gator."

Before he could protest too much further, she made a beeline for her vehicle parked a few rows over from where they'd been sitting.

"Hey, Dax," Toby called. "Can we set up that meeting now?"

Fucking wonderful. "Sure."

Toby pointed toward the middle of the lot. "TJ, go to my truck," he said to his son. "I'll be there in a sec."

"Sure thing, Dad."

Dax stuffed his hands in his pockets and strolled toward Toby. "I don't really want to talk here at the rink."

"I thought maybe tomorrow night we could grab a beer at the brewery around seven."

"I can do that," Dax said.

"TJ told me the things you said to him before and during the game." Toby ran a hand across the top of his head. "He really believes you want him on your team. That you're trying to help him."

"I can't comment on that and you know it."

Toby nodded. "I want to say I appreciate what you did out there with my boy." He glanced over his shoulder. "Legacies are often hard to break and you know what I went through with my pop."

Charlie was a real hard-ass. Always riding Toby's ass and often for no good reason.

"Anyway, you showed me that my son is better than me and in a good way. I can appreciate that."

Dax wasn't sure if he totally believed the words tumbling from Toby's mouth, but it was a start. "TJ's a good hockey player. But he's singularly focused."

"I know. I've always wanted him to be better than me. To have a better shot than me. I was always in your fucking shadow."

Dax had heard that a million times. And not just from Toby. There were other kids on other teams that felt the same way. So did their parents. Some families took their boys to play for different teams just because Dax was playing. Being one of the best wasn't always great. It was lonely at the top sometimes. Especially as a kid.

"I push him to stand out and he's got really soft hands. His puck handling is his best attribute."

"But his weakest link is reading the ice," Dax said. "That's what I was working on with him today." That and leadership, but Dax left that out of the statement. No one was ready for TJ to be an actual leader. That may never happen. Not at a real captain level. But he needed to learn to lead his line when he was on the ice. His teammates didn't have his respect. Or his trust because he was a puck hog.

"I've coached my son for ten years. It's hard to all of a sudden not be able to be on the bench," Toby said.

"Can I give you a piece of advice?" Dax dared to ask. Especially now that Serena wasn't anywhere to be seen.

"Sure, but mind you, this doesn't make us friends and it's also not what I want to talk to you about tomorrow."

"That's fair. But what I'm going to say will probably piss you off," Dax said.

"You have a tendency to do that anyway."

Dax laughed. "Stop coaching him. Stop yelling in the stands. Sit quietly and watch the game. Even if the coach is doing something stupid and you know it, don't say anything during the game and don't undermine the coach in front of TJ."

"I always hated it when parents did that to me." Toby nodded. "They say you can't teach an old dog new tricks. Maybe that's not true." He turned on his heel and headed toward his pickup.

Well, that was interesting.

And now he was going to a bar tomorrow with Toby.

Hopefully Dax wouldn't regret that decision.

Weezer

"Get your ass back in bed, you stubborn old fool." Weezer stood in the doorway of the master bedroom of her family home. It had been a long time since she and her husband—technically her ex-husband—lived under the same roof. No one understood their relationship, not that it mattered because they did and it worked for them. "The doctor said you needed to rest for a good forty-eight hours. It hasn't even been twenty-four."

But ever since Malbec had returned and the secret about how the River family had really come to own the River Winery had been brought to light, it was time for all parts of her family to heal.

That meant Carter moving home.

"I'm fine." Carter touched the back of his head and groaned. "I have a touch of a headache. That's all."

"You passed out right there in the middle of town. I was scared shitless. I thought you'd gone and died right in front of me."

"I got a little dizzy from being dehydrated and too much sun. That's all."

"And now you have a mild concussion." She set down the tray of food she'd brought up for dinner. "I seriously thought you had a heart attack and gone and died on me. I even called all the kids and told them I thought it was your heart."

He laughed.

"That's not funny."

"Yeah. It is. My ticker is just fine. Especially now that I'm back living here full-time. Where I belong." He fluffed the pillows before leaning back and taking the tray.

She'd prepared him a healthy dinner of chicken breasts, roasted vegetables, and brown rice. Of course, she'd put her dinner on the tray too.

He smiled like a big kid as she pulled out the second tray from under the bed and joined him. "A man could get used to this."

"Well, don't. You know I will never do all the cooking."

He chuckled. "Yes, dear."

"I'm so glad you agreed to cancel Sunday dinner with the family today." She sliced into her chicken. It wasn't anywhere near as tender as what Carter would have made. She plopped a piece on her tongue and chewed. She was pleasantly surprised. The flavor was excellent.

"I hated doing that about as much as I hate being confined to this bed without it being about making whoopee, but I don't think I could have handled it. We'll have just as much fun next weekend and Dax will be all done with his hockey recruitment, so there won't be any worry about whether or not he will actually show up."

"They look good together," Weezer said.

"I can't agree more, but I know our daughter and she's holding back."

"She's scared." Weezer's four oldest children had been through a world of hurt and it had all been Weezer's fault. Well, most of it. She'd been doing what she could to correct and mend fences. She and Malbec were closer than ever and her relationship with Riesling was better than it ever was.

Weezer had a long way to go with Merlot, though she wasn't quite sure why he was still so pissed off. There were no ex-girlfriends that Weezer had chased away. Both she and Carter had supported Merlot when he switched careers and became a parole officer after Caleb was accused of a crime he didn't commit and was all but chased out of town.

Weezer's blood still boiled over that one. Caleb was a good man. He wouldn't hurt a fly. Not unless he'd been backed into a corner and had been left with no choice but to come out swinging.

Of course, Zinfandel, her baby, every once in a while got pissy with her, blaming her for taking away her older siblings when she'd been a toddler.

Weezer always found that one humorous because Zinfandel had a great relationship with all her siblings and always had. That was the one thing Weezer never interfered with. She always allowed her children to mingle among themselves, even when she'd taken herself out of the equation.

God, she'd been such an idiot.

"I understand that, but if she can't see that one of the reasons Dax came back to Candlewood Falls was for her, then I don't know how she'll ever open up to him, and then she'll lose him again," Carter said. "She's really good at pushing people away."

"Unfortunately, she gets that from me."

Carter leaned over and kissed Weezer's temple. "Maybe so, but you're also really good at bringing everyone back together."

"Thank you for saying that."

"It's true. We're all here. And truth be told, no one ever really left. Malbec might have been living in Napa Valley, but he was always waiting for you to tell him he could come home. Same goes for Riesling and Chablis."

"So what do we do about Dax and Chablis?"

"Nothing." Carter raised a brow.

"You know I can't sit on the sidelines." Weezer pushed her tray to the foot of the bed and shifted. "Did you see the look on Chablis' face when Serena mentioned having to tell the world something that Chablis did?"

"Oh no, Weezer. Don't you dare go there." Carter glared. It was rare that he gave her that look where his forehead crinkled and his eyes narrowed. It was the look he gave their children when he was warning them not to do something that would get them into the kind of trouble they might not be able to get out of.

"I asked you a question, Carter. Could you please answer it?" Weezer arched a brow.

"Yes. I saw the look on Chablis' face. That doesn't mean there is anything there."

"Please," Weezer said. "You know our daughter better than that. And whatever it is, Chablis believes it will either hurt Dax or embarrass him. I have to find out what they think they know and make sure they don't use it."

"If you meddle in her life, she'll push you away and we just got her back. Is that what you want?"

"Of course not. But she and Dax deserve a second chance and they won't get it if people like Alison Weatherby and Serena Tillman are meddling. All I'm doing is fighting fire with fire."

"All that does is make a bigger flame." Carter tapped the side of his head. "Be smart about this. If you really feel the need to get involved, don't do it by being sneaky. Do it by going right to the source. You know Serena. She'll give up the goods if she thinks it will get her what she wants and that's a spot on the team for her son."

"Oh. That's good. If I can tell her I know how to guarantee TJ—"

"Weezer," Carter said sternly. "That's not where I was going."

"But that's where I landed."

11

CHABLIS

Chablis found herself sitting by the picture window with the light on, a book in hand, waiting for Dax. She'd checked her cell five times in the last twenty minutes. It was pushing ten and he still wasn't home. Of course, his house was on the other corner, so she wouldn't see the headlights to his car anyway.

The last game ended at nine and she knew he wanted to watch that one. The rink was a half hour away. He should be pulling in any second.

Of course, some of his old high school buddies could have talked him into going out for beers. He'd been asked a dozen times at the parade. And she knew his family wanted to spend time with him. It was crazy to think he would want to spend all his free time with her. Besides, she didn't have the energy to have the most important conversation of her life tonight.

Nor would she be able to say no to him once he started kissing her.

She groaned. Her real motivation for wanting Dax to come over was purely physical. Their last encounter out by the river's edge hadn't been enough. It was simply the first taste. A teaser to what could be if only she let him back in her life completely.

She closed the book, pushed to a standing position, and padded across the family room, flipping off the light switch on the wall. All she had to do was turn off the one outside and in the kitchen. Before she did that, she wanted to get a water. She ducked her head into the fridge.

Ding. Dong.

She jumped. The book slipped from her fingertips and landed with a thud on her feet. "Shit, that hurt." She closed the refrigerator and glanced over her shoulder.

Dax stood at the back door with a big goofy smile on his face.

She bent over, picked up her novel, and set it on the counter before opening the door for Dax. "I thought you were going to text first."

"My cell died and I didn't have a charger with me." He stepped into the kitchen and pulled her into his arms. "I saw the light on, so I walked over." He planted his warm lips on hers in a kiss that felt like it belonged in the bedroom. A twinge of guilt tugged at her heartstrings. She wasn't using him for pleasure. It wasn't like she planned on kicking him to the curb.

No.

She wanted to start something special with him. Something that would last a lifetime.

He lifted her off her feet.

"Whoa. What are you doing?"

"Do you really have to ask?" He carried her down the short hallway and into her bedroom where he laid her down on the mattress. He stood at the end of the bed and took off his shirt.

She bit down on her lower lip as she stared at his six-pack abs.

"I've been preoccupied thinking about getting naked with you for the last few hours."

"That's not fair to the kids trying out for your team." Her words were meant tongue in cheek, and she hoped he took them that way. She knew he took his job as coach of the CFW Prep elite hockey team seriously. This was the next chapter in his life.

"What's not fair is that you're not taking your clothes off." He lowered his jeans over his hips.

She believed what he'd told her earlier about wanting to start over in Candlewood Falls. It was important to her that he'd come back for himself. That she wasn't his sole motivation.

"I'm enjoying watching you right now." She scooted to the top of the bed, shimmying out of her sweatpants, and leaned against the headboard, wearing only her shirt and panties.

"Take your shirt off," he said with a deep throaty growl.

"You're so demanding." She ripped it over her head and tossed it at him.

He laughed. "Now the bra and underwear." He kicked his pants to the side and pulled back one side of the sheets before stepping out of his boxers and climbing into bed.

Being with him was easy. Natural. It felt like home. And that scared her.

Forgiving her for what she'd done seventeen years ago should be a formality. At least that's what she told herself. Or what she wanted to believe. They were barely adults when she'd made that decision and he'd told her more than once that if she hadn't pushed him away at the times she had, he would have done it.

Which is exactly what he did the final time they'd seen each other before she'd made the decision that changed the course of her life forever.

She palmed his cheek and stared deep into his blue-green eyes. She could see right into the depths of his soul. He had such a tender heart when he showed it, which wasn't often and only to a select few.

She'd been lucky that he'd chosen to share it with her at all. He'd always been guarded as a kid, keeping his emotions close to the vest. He told her that he saved everything for the ice. For the game. That all his desire and passion went from his brain to his skates to his stick.

And occasionally to her.

Or so he'd tease.

But it was actually a true statement.

His world had been hockey and she was thrilled that she got to watch his career take off. That she'd loved him and herself enough to know they both had things they needed to do before they could get to this place.

She smiled. "I'm glad you came back."

"Tonight or in general?"

"Both." She pushed him to his back and kissed the center of his chest. Her fingers glided across his stomach, which twitched under her touch. She loved the way his muscles flexed.

When she'd agreed to come home, her father had told her that life had a way of coming full circle. She'd watched her parents divorce and then have three more kids while living in two different houses. They had never stopped loving each other.

Never.

Chablis had always loved Dax. Only she had to do it from a distance.

He pooled her hair on the top of her head while she took him intimately into her mouth.

His thigh muscles tightened.

She loved teasing him this way. More so than any other man she'd ever been with. Perhaps it was because he'd been her first everything.

And she'd been his.

They'd taught each other how to kiss. Touch. Explore.

The only difference between then and now was age and experience.

He tugged at her hair, bringing her lips to his, kissing her hard as he filled her in every way.

She couldn't imagine being with anyone else ever again. It was as if they hadn't actually been separated for seventeen years. They fit together. Not just physically, but emotionally and every other way that mattered.

They were connected.

Her life had come full circle and this was exactly where she belonged.

In his arms.

In his bed.

This was her man.

He thrust his hips and she arched into him, wrapping her legs around his, holding him tight.

Her climax slowly began to build. Her breathing became ragged. Her muscles burned with desire. Her toes curled as she held on to every sensation.

"Chablis," he whispered. "I love you."

Her orgasm tore through her body like a fighter jet taking off from an aircraft carrier. It soared high and revved hard. Her body quivered as she accepted his exploding climax. The words she so desperately felt formed in her mind and trickled to her lips.

"I love you too," she managed to croak out. Her heart lurched to her throat. There was no going back now. Saying it not only made it real, but it solidified her commitment to giving their relationship a second chance.

A real chance.

He rolled to his side and pulled the covers over their bodies. "Care to repeat that?"

"No," she said, resting her head on his chest. "Next time we have a sleepover, I want to stay in the main house."

He laughed. "We can do that tomorrow night on one condition."

"What's that?"

"You say you love me again." He kissed her nose.

"That's blackmail."

"Yup."

She tilted her head. Her chest tightened. She wasn't going to ruin the moment with the pains of the past. They loved each other. He'd understand. She knew he would. She'd tell him tomorrow.

"I love you," she said.

"Does this mean I can tell everyone that we're officially back together? Because I'm tired of listening to the gossip and telling people were just friends."

She laughed. "Why do we have to announce it? Why can't we just be together and let everyone else figure it out?"

"That's fair, but we have to at least tell our families."

She groaned. "My mother's going to want to throw a party."

"My mom's going to start planning the wed—"

"Bite your tongue." She playfully slapped his stomach. She wasn't ready for that discussion. "Maybe we don't tell them either. They will make such a big deal about it."

"Whatever makes you happy." He sighed. "But we better get some shut-eye. My alarm is going off at six."

"Why?"

"First game I need to see is at eight."

"Don't these kids have school?" she asked.

"Spring break," he said. "It's why they do the showcase this week. Once it's done, I'll have my list, and admissions will have made all their decisions. I'll know by next week who has accepted my offer and if I need to extend it to a second choice, but I don't think that will happen. I know the kids who have CFW as their first choice. If they are a good fit, I want to give them the opportunity."

"You're a good man." She yawned. "I'm coming with you." She wondered if maybe she should wait until after tryouts to tell him her secret.

What was one more week?

Every time Dax drove by the brewery his cheeks heated. Seeing his face displayed on the side of the building along with all his hockey accomplishments was both humbling and thrilling at the same time. He parked his vehicle and made his way to the door, trying to ignore the larger-than-life-size portrait, but it was impossible.

"Axel did a great job," Toby said, coming up behind him. "You had quite the career."

"Thanks." He opened the door, letting Toby step in first.

Thankfully, the bar wasn't too crowded. Dax found a table at the back of the bar. A waiter greeted them quickly and they ordered a pitcher of draft beer and the sharable apps.

"I appreciate you taking the time to meet with me tonight," Toby said.

"I'm going to get a lot of shit for it if any of the other parents find out."

"They won't hear it from me." Toby raised his glass.

"I know this is going to sound rude, but your wife is going to blab it." Dax had to admit, he was thrilled beyond belief that Serena hadn't been at the rink all day. There were a lot of annoying voices in the stands, but none as annoying as hers. And of course, she always managed to corner him when he least expected it.

"She doesn't know I'm here."

Dax glanced over his shoulder. "This is a small town. People talk. I'm sure it will get back to Serena that we sat down and had a beer. Besides, won't she wonder where you are?" Dax raised his beer to his lips.

"Serena moved out of the house this past weekend."

Dax coughed. "Shit, man. I'm sorry." He might have had issues with Toby and his wife, but he didn't wish that kind of trouble on anyone.

"It's been a long time coming, but I don't want TJ to be caught in the middle of something that has nothing to do with him, and Serena doesn't fight fair."

That was an understatement. Dax remembered all the crazy stunts Serena pulled back in the day. He'd watched Toby and Serena get together, break up, and get back together all through high school until their junior year. There was a long period of time where Serena had been out of the picture, but Dax had heard they got back together sometime right after college, but he honestly didn't pay much attention. He'd been too busy with his career and trying to forget about Chablis.

"Before we go any further," Toby continued, "I want to apologize to you for being an asshole. You and I were never friends. As a kid, I was a bit of a dick."

"Your words. Not mine."

Toby laughed. "I believe you called me that a few times."

"I might have."

"I know TJ has a chip on his shoulder where hockey is concerned and I also get that's partly my fault. I tried so hard to build him up, instead of cutting him down. Growing up, my dad always compared me to you. If only I had your speed. Your soft hands. If only I could read the ice like you did. And the sad part is that it started when we were like six."

"That pretty much breaks my heart." Dax always knew that Charlie had been hard on his kid, but hearing it from Toby changed the way he looked at the situation.

"Do you remember when I was accused of tampering with your skate blades?"

"That was Serena, but I assumed you had something to do with it."

Toby shook his head. "I found out recently that my dad paid her to do it."

"Are you shitting me?"

"I wish I were."

The waiter interrupted for a few moments to set a large platter of appetizers on the center of the table.

"When I went to college, I was done with Serena," Toby said as he loaded up his plate with some greasy food. "Mind you, I only knew of some of the things she'd done, but I had no idea my dad was behind them. All I wanted to do was play hockey without being in your shadow and for four years I did exactly that and it was fucking awesome."

"I'm glad," Dax said, taking a cheeseburger slider and popping it into his mouth. Damn, he was hungry.

"I had no intention of coming back to this town after I graduated, but my dad got sick and my mom begged, so I did. For the next few years all I did was work and deal with my dying father who did nothing but tell me what a shit I was while he watched your NHL career take off. Right before Serena came back to town." Toby's eyes glossed over. He glanced toward the ceiling. "She'd been through some shit and needed a shoulder to cry on. I was an old, familiar face."

Dax nibbled on a few cheesy fries and sipped his beer while he let Toby purge his story. Dax had no idea where it was going or why he needed to listen to it, but he wasn't going to interrupt the man.

"She'd been in a bad relationship and she'd just found out she was pregnant with TJ."

"Wait. What?" Dax set his beer on the table and stared at Toby.

"Biologically, TJ isn't mine. He knows that. I

adopted him when he was born," Toby said. "We never lied to him about that."

"Wow." Dax didn't know what else to say.

"Serena was a broken girl when she came back here. Her ex did a real number on her, and her parents—no, her father—had cut her off."

"But they are so close."

"Now. But they weren't then, and it took TJ to bring them back together." Toby ran his thumb and forefinger across his chin. "For a while, she'd changed. She was sweet and kind, and I'd fallen madly in love with this new, improved version. And for a few years things were good. Real good. We were happy."

"What happened?"

"She had an affair," Toby said. "With TJ's biological father."

"Jesus. When?" Dax shook his head. "Sorry. I shouldn't have asked that question. It's none of my business."

"No. It's fair. It started a few months ago. I just recently found out. But for the record, I haven't told anyone why she left."

"She didn't take TJ?" Dax shoved his plate aside and folded his hands on the table.

"No. He's staying with me. But that's a long, complicated story." Toby leaned back and blew out a puff of air. "I need to do what's best for my son. There is no way I'm going to be able to keep his mother's affair a secret from him forever. He's already asking questions. I wanted to wait until this tryout process was over, but Serena's threat about Chablis pushed me over the edge, and when I confronted her, I basically gave her an ultimatum."

Dax swallowed. Hard. "What does Chablis have to do with any of this?"

"I don't know," Toby said. "I wish I did. But Serena and her mother have both hinted more than once that they know something about Chablis that is so damning that it will destroy both your reputations."

"I can't imagine what that could be," Dax said. "And I don't like being threatened."

"I'm sure you don't and it's why I'm telling you all of this." Toby leaned forward. "I will admit I didn't like the idea of you coaching the CFW Prep team. You're changing my mind real quick. And my son likes you."

"He's a good kid."

"Thanks. I appreciate that," Toby said. "TJ is one of the best things that has ever happened to me and I want to do right by him. I can't do that if I'm behaving like a jealous child myself and truth be told, when I learned you were going to be the new coach, I thought fucking wonderful. My wife is cheating on me and now I have to deal with all my old teenage inadequacies all over again."

"We were kids. What the hell did we know."

"You knew exactly what you wanted and nothing was going to stop you."

"I had no idea if I was good enough," Dax said.

"When I got up to Canada, I was just some kid from Jersey who played on the third line."

Toby laughed. "I can't imagine you not being the star."

"In a weird way, it was really nice," Dax admitted. "I didn't have the pressure of staying on top anymore. But I had to work harder to get noticed. And I was scared it was all going to end there."

"I'd say you should come play in my men's league, but I get enough shit about how good I am. Imagine what they'd say if you showed up," Toby said. "Of course, they'd make us play against each other."

"Now that might actually be fun."

Toby lifted his hand and waggled a finger. "I don't think so, but getting back to my situation and Chablis." He lifted the pitcher and filled both their glasses. "I have proof of my wife's affair. Like picture proof. We also have a prenup, so she knows she's not getting much from me. But what scares me is what she might try to do to you."

"Why?" Dax struggled with why Toby felt the need to unleash all his problems onto Dax, though it was helpful to understand what his son was going through.

"Brooks Halsteder—"

"I know Brooks," Dax said. His pulse kicked up a notch. He hadn't heard Brooks' name in many years. Brooks was someone Dax hoped he never ran into again. Their last encounter had ended with Dax losing his temper.

It was rare that happened, but Brooks didn't like Dax and as a college referee, Brooks made it his life mission to keep Dax in the penalty box.

Dax got tired of it and so did his coach. They went to the referee board and Brooks was removed.

At least from the division one schedule.

"Not well. But our paths have crossed a few times. He was also up for the CFW Prep coaching job."

"He's TJ's biological father."

"That's fucked up." Dax ran a hand over the top of his head. "Does TJ know any of this?"

"We never told TJ who his dad was, just that I adopted him. Serena has threatened to tell him, which is one of the reasons he's staying with me. But I'm not going to be able to control this narrative forever," Toby said. "And I'm sure she wants you gone so Brooks can come in and take your job. She's just waiting for the right time to reveal whatever she thinks she has on you or Chablis."

"There's nothing there." Dax's chest tightened. Chablis had been wanting to tell him something about her past.

Every time she brought it up, she got teary-eyed.

Whatever it was, it couldn't be something that would cause him to lose his job.

"Well, watch your back, because now that Serena knows I'm on team Dax and fully supportive of TJ playing for you, she's going to go ballistic."

"I appreciate the heads-up." Dax pulled out his wallet.

"Let me get this," Toby said.

"I can't let you do that."

Toby held up his hands. "I'm not going to argue with you."

"I'll see you at the rink tomorrow." Dax stood, holding out his hand. "And listen. If you ever need someone to talk to, give me a call."

"Thanks. Say hello to Chablis for me."

"Will do." Time to have that conversation with Chablis.

Dax

Dax pulled into his garage and put his vehicle in park, shutting off the engine. He took the manila envelope someone had stuffed in his mailbox and stared at the handwritten words: *To Dax Fabion.*

He slipped from behind the steering wheel and made his way inside the house. "Chablis? Are you here?"

"In the family room," she called. "I opened a bottle of wine. It's in the kitchen. I also brought over some cheese and crackers. They are in here with me."

"I'll be right in." He found the wine and poured a

small glass. His day was going to start bright and early again, but at least tomorrow the last game he needed to watch would be at two. However, he had a meeting to attend at CFW Prep at four, so it would still be a long day.

He ripped open the envelope and pulled out what looked like medical papers. It wasn't too thick. Maybe ten pages.

A sticky note was taped to the top.

Did you know about this?

Well, shit. He took a big gulp of wine before scanning the documents, looking for the patient name.

Chablis River.

The paperwork was dated seventeen years ago. And it was from a women's clinic two towns away.

Patient is eleven weeks pregnant. An induced abortion was performed. No complications at time of discharge. Patient is to return in two weeks for a follow-up. Patient will return if bleeding or pain does not subside.

He set the wine down. His stomach churned. He lifted the papers and took them into the family room. He couldn't decide if he was angry, sad, or somewhere in between. A numbness filled his muscles and a fog entered his brain. He stood in front of Chablis and opened his mouth, but nothing came out.

"What's wrong?" She untucked her feet and moved to the edge of the sofa. "Did something happen between you and Toby?"

Dax shook his head. He squeezed the papers in his

hand as the reality of what he'd just found out hit his mind.

She'd been pregnant.

With what he assumed was his baby.

And she chose not to tell him about it.

"Why didn't you tell me?" he asked.

"Tell you what?" Chablis tilted her head. She reached for the papers in his hand.

He released them.

She brought them to her face and gasped. "Where did you get these?"

"Someone put them in my mailbox." He folded his arms and turned toward the picture window. "I literally just opened it."

"This is what I wanted to talk to you about," she said with a shaky voice. "But this is not how I wanted you to find out."

"I suppose not."

"These are personal medical records. Whoever obtained these and gave them to you did something illegal." She sniffled.

"We'll deal with that." He knew how cold he sounded, but he couldn't help it. His emotions were all over the place and he couldn't get past the fact that she'd chosen to keep this from him all these years.

But more so these last few days. Especially after he'd told her he loved her. That should have been enough for her to tell him something this big.

And then there was the fact she'd gone through this alone.

Or maybe she hadn't.

That thought made his blood boil.

"I was going to tell you tonight," she said.

"That doesn't make me feel any better." He rubbed the back of his neck as he tried to unjumble all the thoughts rumbling around in his brain. He tried to keep from allowing his emotions to take over. He wanted to remain levelheaded and not lose his cool. That was the last thing that Chablis needed. "You should have told me this at the very latest last night." He turned.

She sat cross-legged on the sofa with the papers in her trembling hands. Tears strolled down her cheeks. "Last night was a big deal. I didn't want to ruin our moment." She swiped at her face. "And to be honest, I was scared."

He pinched the bridge of his nose. "Of what? Of me?"

"Of your reaction." She set the papers on the sofa. "I made a decision, which I don't regret, but once you and I started getting close again, I knew I needed to tell you."

"But you didn't."

"After our conversation about how each of us was happy with the way our lives played out, I thought it could wait."

He meandered around the coffee table and sat down

on the couch. He took her hand and ran his thumb over the back side. "You were pregnant when you came to see me in Buffalo and I turned you away."

"I was," she said.

"Were you going to tell me about the baby that night?" He held his breath for a moment. He wasn't sure how he wanted her to answer. "Was having an abortion always the plan? Or did you want to keep it if I had been receptive to you wanting to get back together?"

She pulled her knees to her chest. "I wanted to at least have the conversation."

"But again, you didn't." He bolted to his feet. "Damn it, Chablis. You should have told me back then. And you should have told me before—you just should have fucking told me. And now Serena knows and she's going to use this to try and hurt us."

"She obviously already has," Chablis whispered. "I'm not making excuses. But I was young. And scared. I had no one. My brother had run off to Napa Valley. Riesling was on and off with her ex. Merlot had switched majors and colleges. I felt alone."

"Who knows about the abortion?"

"Malbec. He was with me."

"Fucking asshole," Dax mumbled.

"Why are you mad at him? What the hell did he do?"

"He knew and didn't tell me. All these years, he could have reached out. He should have called me before he drove you to the clinic. I had the right to know. I should have been the one there holding your hand."

She arched a brow. "You agree with what I did."

"That didn't come out right," he said. "I would have supported you, but yeah. I do. We had no business becoming parents at that point in our lives." His mind went back to the conversation he'd had earlier with Toby and how Toby had stepped up to adopt and raise another man's child. That took real maturity.

"I didn't want you to," she said.

He lowered his chin. "Why the fuck not?"

"You said it yourself. When I was in your life, I was a distraction. I realized that day you sent me away that I wasn't good for you."

"Are you kidding me? You're the love of my life." He inhaled sharply. He needed to fill his lungs with oxygen.

"Maybe so," she said. "But if I had told you I was pregnant, what would you have done? And before you answer that, I want you to really think about your answer."

An image of her with a round belly flashed in his mind.

It had to be the most intoxicating picture he'd ever seen.

"I probably would have gotten on bended knee and asked you to marry me." He made his way back to the sofa. "I'm sorry I blew up at you. This threw me for a loop."

"I had an entire speech worked out."

He wrapped his arm around her shoulder and pulled her close. "Toby told me that Serena was coming for us."

"How would Serena get my medical records—oh, her mom's a nurse."

"Where does she work?"

"I have no idea," Chablis said. "But I'm sure Serena did this."

"So am I." Dax kissed Chablis' temple. "Come. Let's go to bed. We'll deal with all this tomorrow when we're fresh."

"You don't hate me for what I did?"

"I'm not happy that you didn't tell me, but as far as the abortion goes, no. However, I wouldn't want you to have one now. I'd like to have at least one kid. Maybe two."

She lowered her chin and arched a brow.

"I'm serious. I love you. I want a family and I'm not getting any younger." He tilted her chin with his thumb and forefinger. She was his world and he could no longer imagine life without her in it. He would do whatever it took to make sure no one destroyed their second chance.

Not even Brooks.

13

WEEZER

Weezer sat in her favorite chair in her family room and stared at the medical records. Tears welled in her eyes.

Her poor baby girl.

The things her children had to endure because of a secret she thought was better kept buried.

A legacy she'd passed on to her older kids.

A scorching pain tore through her heart. "I'm so sorry, Chablis. Dax." She glanced up and shifted her gaze between her daughter and the man she loved, who sat on the sofa across from her, holding hands, and her husband who leaned against the fireplace. "This is all my fault."

"No. It's not," Chablis said. "Dax and I couldn't have survived back then and we both know it."

"She's right." Dax nodded. "We've talked through

217

all of this. What Chablis did isn't the issue. We're at peace with that. But what someone is trying to do to us —to me and my career—that's the problem."

"I'm glad you called the police," Carter said.

"Alison Weatherby is a lot of things, but it's hard for me to believe she'd steal your medical records like that." Weezer set the papers aside and leaned back. She'd known Alison since grade school. Alison was the type of girl who always wanted more. She had to be the best and have the best.

It had surprised Weezer when Alison became a nurse. She never thought the woman could have a decent bedside manner. But Alison barely worked with patients. She was always on the management or administration side of things. Alison prided herself in being a great leader.

Her staff thought otherwise.

And she raised an entitled child.

Of course, who was Weezer to talk.

Weezer made a shit ton of mistakes with her kids and it wasn't easy to fix them. But at least she was trying.

She couldn't say the same for Alison.

"The officer who took our statement this morning said they were going to go to the clinic today and question anyone who worked there when Chablis had the procedure," Dax said.

"We all know that would be Alison," Carter said. "She's worked there for twenty-five years."

"I'm sure there's other staff too," Weezer added. "What I don't understand is how would exposing this benefit them?"

Dax ran a hand over the top of his head. "In order to answer that question fully, I have to break a confidence when it comes to Toby and also tell you something from my past that I'm not necessarily proud of."

Chablis tilted her head. "Something I don't know?"

Dax nodded.

Weezer didn't like the sound of that.

Dax stood, taking his glass of lemonade, and moved toward the picture window that overlooked the vineyard.

Whatever troubled that young man, troubled Weezer's daughter, and that meant it was Weezer's problem. She scurried across the room and sat next to Chablis, taking her hand.

"Why do you care about Toby?" Weezer asked. "He's never been very kind to you."

"Did you know that TJ wasn't his biological son?" Dax asked.

"I knew that," Carter said. "I did the paperwork for him. It was a closed adoption. And I don't know how many people in town know."

"Everyone believes they got married because Serena was pregnant." Weezer had a horrible habit of jumping to conclusions in her younger days. This was one of those times she probably shouldn't have since adopting another man's child in that kind of situation was a decent thing to do. "So, that's not true."

"Not in the way people in this town believe, but that's only part of the picture," Dax said.

Weezer let her mind go back to the time when Chablis had left town. It was one of the hardest periods in Weezer's life. She had three little children underfoot. Her husband was living across town and she was holding on to a secret that was slowly destroying her world, but she couldn't see it. She truly believed that she was saving her family.

She wasn't paying too much attention to everyone else at the time. Or at least as much as she usually did.

"What's the rest?" Carter asked.

"TJ's biological father is someone I know. Someone who has an even bigger reason to destroy my career than Toby or Serena do," Dax said.

"And who is he and why does he matter?" Chablis squeezed Weezer's hand harder.

"His name is Brooks Halsteder. He used to be a college ref. Before that, I played with him on an elite summer team."

"So, Toby played with him?" Carter asked.

"No. It was an older team that I played on. I was two or three years younger than everyone," Dax said. "If I thought Toby had issues with me, this man's sole purpose was to take me out of the game. It got so bad that me and my college coaches had to take drastic measures to have him removed."

"I take it you were successful," Carter said.

Dax nodded. "He was banned from reffing division one games, but allowed to drop down to division three and high school. After that, he threatened me a few times. We got physical at a party once. Cops were called. We both ended up in the hospital. It was a mess. But he ended up getting arrested because he came at me with a knife. He blamed me for ruining his career—no, his life. My coaches told me to not look back. To not think about him or what happened. Because I didn't do anything wrong. All I did was defend myself."

"Your coaches were right," Carter said.

"How come we never heard about any of this?" Chablis said.

"The school did their best to keep it under wraps," Dax said. "My family never pressed charges, so he walked away. Until now, I had no idea what happened to him."

"So, what does he want?" Weezer asked.

"For starters, my job," Dax said. "But I suspect he's trying to destroy my reputation and my life." He pointed toward the papers that Weezer had left on her chair. "He and Serena, who are having an affair—but that's not to be repeated—probably thought that by exposing what Chablis did might send me packing. Or maybe embarrass both of us, if they go public."

"That would be cruel." Weezer wrapped her arm around her little girl. "I would hate for you to be publicly humiliated like that."

"It's nobody else's business, but I really don't care what other people think," Chablis said.

"I'm more concerned about the fact someone violated her privacy." Dax set his drink on the coffee table. "In that same vein, I want to make sure that TJ and Toby are protected. I don't want them to be hurt by anything we choose to do in order to deal with whatever Serena and Brooks toss at me and Chablis."

"You're a good man, Dax." Carter strolled across the room and squeezed his shoulder. "We'll do whatever we can, but I'm not going to stand here and let anyone hurt my family. And you're family."

"I appreciate that." Dax gave a short nod.

"Besides going after Alison legally, what else are you planning?" Weezer ran her hand up and down Chablis' back. "Because we can sit here and play defense."

"We agree, Mom," Chablis said. "I'm going to be at the rink every day with Dax. We're heading there as soon as we leave here."

"Brooks is coaching an elite travel team that will be playing in the showcase tournament this week," Dax said. "He doesn't have any kids on the roster that I'm looking at, which is why I never saw his name."

"Poor Toby. Did he know this man was going to be there this week?" Weezer asked. She'd always had a bigger problem with Serena, but she'd treated Toby poorly over the years. In part, because sometimes he deserved it, but maybe, like her, he'd been misunderstood.

"Not until I told him," Dax said. "I don't want to be sitting around waiting for whatever bullshit they have planned. I want to go on the offensive and I know how to push his buttons. But it might not be pretty, and I wanted to bring the two of you into the loop."

"Thank you for that," Carter said. "However, why do I get the feeling that I'm also here as legal counsel?"

"It's not really like that. But I do want to make sure my contract with the school is buttoned down. I don't want any surprises."

"Is there a morality clause?" Weezer asked.

Dax nodded.

"That's a nonissue," Carter said. "Dax didn't have the procedure. Chablis did. I could easily fight that and win. Anything else the school could nail you on?"

"A few barroom brawls, but no arrests that stuck," Dax said. "I'm sure Brooks has more skeletons than I do and I've contacted an old friend to dig them up."

"I want that friend's number," Carter said.

Weezer loved it when her husband got into work mode. He was the best lawyer, in her eyes, in the state of New Jersey. He was kind and he cared about his clients. He bent over backward to make sure the people he worked for got the best attention and representation possible.

"Brooks will be at the rink today," Chablis said.

"The police are headed to the clinic as we speak. We need to get the ball rolling on this."

"If we can get Brooks backed into a corner, he'll come out swinging and that's never a good look on him," Dax said. "All I want to do is make sure that TJ is protected. Which leaves me with one last favor."

"What's that?" Carter asked.

"The adoption and a father's rights," Dax said. "Will you represent Toby not only in a divorce, but in a custody battle? And what do you think his chances are in keeping custody of a child that's not his biologically if the biological father is in the picture?"

"First. I'd be happy to represent him," Carter said. "Second. If Alison did steal Chablis' records, that will get her prison time. If Serena knew about it, that's also criminal. That will make his case stronger, but only if he didn't know about it."

"He didn't," Dax said with conviction. "When I called him this morning, he was shocked. Actually, mortified was more like it and he's willing to do whatever it takes to help us."

"Good," Carter said. "Tell him to come see me today. I'll give him the friends and family deal. If he gives me a couple hundred today, signs on the dotted line, he's got himself a lawyer."

"He's waiting for my text." Dax stretched out his arm. "Thank you."

Weezer jumped to her feet, pulling Chablis with her. "I know you two need to get going. Please keep us in the loop." She kissed Chablis on the cheek. "And Dax, I'm sorry I meddled all those years ago. I won't do it this time around."

Dax laughed. "I have a feeling that statement isn't entirely true."

14

CHABLIS

Chablis took the cup of hot chocolate that Dax handed her and palmed it with both hands. Her heart hammered in her throat. Her father had texted that he'd been in contact with the police and they were at the clinic.

Which meant Alison knew they were not only onto her, but taking action.

"Chablis. Relax." Dax ran his hands up and down her biceps.

"Serena is here. Once she finds out we're shaking in our boots, she's going to lash out."

"So, do it first." Dax leaned in and pressed his warm lips on her cheek. He let them linger for a long moment.

She leaned into him, soaking up his strength and confidence. "Aren't you concerned at all?"

"Of course I am. I don't like our personal business being displayed for the world to judge."

"How did your parents handle what I did?" She'd been worried about that and wanted to be there with Dax when he told them, but he thought it might be best if he did it alone. His mother had a conservative viewpoint and might need to take a beat to accept it completely.

"I thought my mother was going to get in her car, drive straight to the clinic, and beat the crap out of Alison, she was so pissed at what she did." Dax smiled. "She's sorry for her role in trying to push us apart so I would follow my dream."

"Hard to believe our mothers spent any time speaking to each other back in the day."

Dax laughed. "Yeah. That came as a bit of a shocker. But all that is in the past. We have a fresh start."

Reaching up, she palmed his face. Just a week ago, if anyone had asked her if she thought she and Dax would ever get back together, she would have said absolutely not. That their time had passed.

But today, she knew without a doubt that Dax Fabion was her soulmate. And if she was being honest with herself, she'd known that from the very first kiss.

"I love you," she whispered.

"I love you right back."

"Aw, don't you two look cute." The sound of her baby sister's voice cut through the air.

Chablis jumped. She glanced over her shoulder and saw Zinfandel standing behind her with a fruity drink in her hand. She pushed the straw to her lips and sucked. "Shit, Zinny, you scared me."

"I hate it when you call me that."

Chablis was the only one who still occasionally called the youngest River child by her nickname, and it drove Zinfandel batshit crazy. Which was one of the reasons she did it. But also because sometimes her baby sister acted like a child. Of course, Zinny was about to turn twenty-four, so she was young and still had some maturing to do.

"Don't sneak up on me and I won't," Chablis said. "What are you doing here?"

"Toby called me and asked me to run interference with his soon to be ex," Zinfandel said. "He mentioned something weird might happen today and he wasn't sure if he could be at the rink when it happened. He wanted to make sure TJ didn't see whatever it was."

"Why would he call you?" Dax asked. "I thought he said he was calling his nanny."

Zinfandel pointed to herself. "Not a nanny, but I did babysit that boy from the time he was born and I also still do sometimes if they go away overnight. Though I've never understood why she hired me. She's not a fan of our family. But the pay was good."

"Did you know that?" Dax asked Chablis.

"I guess I thought Toby mentioned it would be my sister."

"Nope. But at least now I know it's someone I can really trust." Dax leaned in and kissed Zinfandel's cheek. "You grew up nice."

"Hey. That's my baby sister." Chablis playfully smacked Dax's shoulder. "She's barely a grown-up."

"She looks like an adult to me." Dax winked.

"Someone might be sleeping alone tonight if he's not careful." Chablis followed Zinfandel out of the small cafe and back toward rink two with Dax right behind them. She stopped at the corner of the rink, where TJ's team was going to be. Currently the Zamboni was cleaning the ice. "Where are you going to be while I watch this game?" she asked Dax. "Brooks' team is playing on rink five right now. His game should be over when TJ's is in the third period."

"Toby told me he sent information to CFW Prep about bar fights you've been in and lawsuits against you. Is any of that true?" Zinfandel asked.

"Yes and no," Dax admitted. "I spoke with the board and they couldn't give me too much, since I'm not officially under review."

"This is ridiculous," Chablis muttered. She couldn't believe how everything had changed in the matter of one day. Between Serena and her mother trying to stir up trouble with Chablis and Dax and now Brooks giving the school information about Dax's questionable character, Chablis wanted to scream.

Better yet, she wanted to rip Serena's hair out strand by strand.

Dax rested his hand on the small of her back. "I'm not worried, so you shouldn't be either."

"But if it's true, can't the school fire you?"

"Not based on the truth," Dax said. "Now the spin Brooks puts on all of it, I look like an out-of-control whack job. But the school board has the two police reports that matter. Once they read them, they will laugh Brooks right out the door."

"They why did he do it?" Zinfandel chewed on her straw.

"He was banking on them seeing I was picked up for a fight and toss me out on my ass," Dax said.

"He never divulged that intel to the school," Chablis added. "He wasn't required to since he wasn't ever actually charged with any wrongdoing, but Brooks made it seem like there was more to the story. However, Dax had a meeting with the board, and they know everything."

"So, why are you confronting him?" Zinfandel asked.

"I'm not," Dax said. "I'm simply making my presence known, while doing my damndest to protect TJ. I don't want that kid to be hurt." He leaned in and kissed Chablis. "I've got to run. I'll talk to you soon. Good to see you, Zinny."

"Haha. Such a funny man."

"I have my moments." Dax turned and waved over his shoulder as headed for the other rink.

"Damn, he's hot." Zinfandel fanned herself. "You are one lucky girl."

"Aren't I though." Chablis smiled. Her heart swelled. Being with Dax again was like jumpstarting her entire world. "I'm glad you're here. You've been so busy lately; I barely see you these days."

"Work is insane and Mom has me learning the books for the winery, which is great, except it's on her terms and you know how that goes."

"I'm happy to help you navigate that." Chablis laughed. "What's Serena going to do when she sees you here?"

"Toby set it up for me to bring TJ home since Serena has a shift at the restaurant. She wasn't thrilled about that. Told him she could swing it, but he made a stink about Brooks being at the rink and how she didn't tell him that he was coming to town and how that could affect their son considering they just split. Blah, blah, blah." Zinfandel glanced over her right shoulder, then her left before she found a trash can and tossed her plastic cup. "Toby's terrified what might happen today. I'm under strict instructions to keep him in the loop on what goes down today. So far, Serena has agreed not to say anything about Brooks being TJ's biological father. She actually told him that Brooks isn't ready to be introduced into his life, but Toby doesn't trust that. So, besides me being his lifeline, I'm supposed to run interference, making sure TJ doesn't cross paths with

Brooks and Serena stays away from Dax, if that's possible."

"That's awfully nice of you to do that," Chablis said. "I didn't realize you and Toby were that close."

"It's been a struggle for him this past year."

"Did you know about the affair?" Chablis turned to her baby sister.

"You can't tell anyone I told you, but yeah. Toby told me as soon as he found out. He didn't know who to talk to, so I was a safe space."

Chablis squeezed her sister's arm. "That's so sweet."

"Toby's really a good man. He's made his fair share of mistakes. He knows that and he's going to try to do better, especially when it comes to TJ," Zinfandel said. "But he's got to get through this part first."

"He will." Chablis nodded as the kids came running out of the locker room. "I'm going to go sit up in the stands. Do you want to sit with me?"

"No, thanks. I'm going to go hang out in the warm area. Besides, Serena will be here soon, and the last thing we need is for her to see us together. That might get her hackles up."

"Good point. I'll talk to you later."

Chablis took her clipboard and made her way to the top of the stands. Her sister disappeared into the snack room area and Dax was nowhere to be seen. Her mood soured the moment Serena came into view.

It got worse when Serena made her way up the stands.

Wonderful.

But she shouldn't be shocked. Dax warned her that this would probably happen and reminded her to keep her cool.

"What are you doing here?" Serena asked as she plopped herself down right next to Chablis. "You don't have a child trying out or playing. You don't have a child."

Interesting choice of words and Chablis had half a mind to tell Serena where to go, but it wasn't worth the battle. "What I'm doing doesn't concern you."

"If you're helping Dax, it most certainly does, especially when it's my kid that you seem to be assessing."

"I'm not assessing anyone. I'm making notes. Dax will be doing the evaluation."

"Oh, really?" Serena's voice screeched. "Well, where is he? Because I don't know how the hell he can do any kind of evaluation if he doesn't watch my kid play."

"He's here. He's running between rinks. He has more than one player to look at."

"Not the point," Serena said. "You don't like me. Nor does Dax, and I think taking that out on my son—"

"You can stop right there." Chablis shifted her body and stiffened her spine. "I'm not playing this game with you, Serena. No one is taking anything out on TJ and what you or your mother or whoever stuffed in Dax's mailbox—well, for your information, we've called the proper authorities to investigate." Chablis' heart dropped to the pit of her stomach. Dax had told her to go ahead and drop the ball if she had the chance. They didn't want this to drag out too long. Besides, it was only a matter of time before the authorities came and questioned Serena about what happened. There was no one else who had any reason to do it.

Or at least no one they had any reason to believe would want to hurt them.

"What on earth are you talking about?" Serena narrowed her eyes and jerked her head back. She looked as though she might have swallowed a lemon.

Whole.

"I don't know what you thought you would accomplish by sending Dax my medical records because the only thing it's going to do is get you in trouble." Chablis fought the tears. Hard. No way would she let this woman see her cry over pain she felt for the choices she'd made. While she didn't regret it, that didn't mean it wasn't one of the most difficult things she'd ever done in her life.

Serena stuck her nose in the air. "I honestly have no clue as to what you are blubbering about."

"You can keep saying that, but your mom still works part-time at the clinic I went to. I bet the police are there asking her questions right now."

Serena's eyes grew wide.

"That's right. If you thought either one of us was

going to take that sitting down, you don't know either one of us well." Chablis stood. She'd had enough. "Leave me and my boyfriend alone. You can't hurt us. And you're not going to get Dax fired, so stop trying."

Dax

Dax glanced at his cell phone. "Shit," he mumbled, staring at the text from Carter. Quickly, he jogged back toward rink two.

He found Chablis standing in the far corner, closer to the coach's side.

"Hey, you." He looped his arm around her shoulders. "Why aren't you sitting in the stands?"

"Serena."

Dax glanced up. His stomach soured.

This wasn't going to be good.

"Where's Zinfandel?"

"In the snack shack, why?"

"We need to get her. The police are on the way. They are going to pick up Serena."

"For questioning?"

Dax shook his head. "No. They're going to arrest her. Your father texted me." He held out his cell. "Her mother claims she didn't take the records and there is no record of them being accessed in the last year. But what is interesting is it turns out that Serena worked in the billing department ten years ago."

"Are you serious? How did we not know that?"

"I have no idea," Dax said.

"Does that mean she's been holding on to my records? Waiting to use them against me? You?"

"Sweetheart, I have no idea. Your father mentioned they both had pictures of your records on both of their phones. I don't know who took them or when, though your dad was told it was Serena. I just know that I can't have TJ playing hockey and possibly watching his mom have handcuffs slapped on her wrists."

"That would suck for TJ." Chablis shook her head. "I know I shouldn't have, but I confronted her about my medical records. She acted like she knew nothing."

Dax's chest tightened. TJ was going to be dealing with some pretty major shit soon and he was going to need a lot of support. Dax knew his family would step up to the plate and it warmed his heart to see Chablis and her family doing the same.

"Did you mention the procedure, or just leaving the records in my mailbox?"

"Just the latter," Chablis said. "I'll get my sister. You should try to get Serena out of the stands."

"That's a good idea," Dax said. "Tell Zinfandel to call Toby and then come find me. I have an idea."

"What's that?"

"Just do it. And hurry. It will be better if this happens as the police get here."

Chablis nodded before taking off for the snack room.

Dax stuffed his hands in his pockets and inhaled sharply. He took the steps two at a time. "Serena. I need to talk with you."

"I'm busy watching my son," she said.

"It's important. Can we step out into the lobby?"

She glanced up and glared. "Why can't you talk right here?"

He offered her his hand. "It's private."

"Are you offering my son a spot on your team?"

If alluding to that got her out of TJ's line of sight, then so be it. "There are some things I need to discuss that I don't need other parents listening to. So if we can take this outside, that would be even better."

"Fine." She hopped to her feet.

Dax followed her through rink one and to the lobby where she paused. Two police cars rolled to a stop in the circle. Dax reached around her and pushed open the door.

"Wait for me," Chablis called as she rushed toward him.

"Why does she need to be at this meeting?" Serena asked with puckered lips.

"Because I have an important question to ask you." Dax raised his hand to the police officer who approached. "Do you want TJ to go to CFW Prep?"

"Of course I do. Why on earth would I let my son

apply if I didn't want him to go?" Serena planted her hands on her hips and glared.

"Do you want me to be his coach?" Dax quickly shifted his gaze to the officer, who thankfully held his ground.

"Do I have any other choice?" Serena asked.

Dax arched a brow. "You're the one who brought Brooks here. You're the one who told him to apply for my job and the two of you are trying to sabotage me and it started when you thought it would be okay to embarrass my girlfriend with her medical records."

Serena shook her head and waggled her finger between Dax and Chablis. "She already accused me of giving you her abortion records. Well, I did no such thing."

Dax waved the police officer over, hoping he'd heard this entire exchange.

"I never said anything about having an abortion," Chablis said behind a tight jaw. "Only that someone gave my medical records to Dax."

"You absolutely told me that," Serena said. "I remember distinctly. I'm sorry that your past indiscretion is catching up to you, but that has nothing to do with me."

"Serena Tillman?" the police officer asked.

"Yes." She narrowed her eyes.

"You have the right to remain silent. Anything you say can and will be used against you—"

"What? Excuse me. You can't do this. What on earth am I being arrested for?" Serena screeched.

"Violation of HIPAA laws, for starters," the officer said.

"I don't know what these two told you, but I didn't do that. How on earth could I have gotten her medical records?" Serena asked.

"Unfortunately for you," the officer began, "your mother has the picture of the records on her phone and the text message that you sent her." The officer continued to read Serena her rights while she yelled a few obscenities at the poor man.

Dax put his arm around Chablis and guided her into the lobby. "This is going to be really hard on TJ and I can only hope that Brooks does the right thing and stays the hell out of his life."

"Did you talk to Brooks?" Chablis asked.

Dax shook his head. "No. I decided it wasn't worth risking a fight. I watched some of the game. I'm sure he saw me. But I walked away."

The door flew open and Toby raced in. "Where's my son?" he asked as he scanned the lobby. "Zinfandel called me and said shit was going down, but then I saw them taking Serena away in the police car. I didn't think it was going to happen that fast."

"He could still be on the ice." Dax checked his watch.

"Or perhaps just getting off. But don't worry. He didn't see anything," Chablis said.

"It's going to be all over the news. I need to get him out of this rink—shit," Dax mumbled as he stared at Brooks strolling through the lobby as if he didn't have a care in the world. "Don't look—"

"What?" Toby glanced over his shoulder. "You fucking asshole," he muttered.

"Keep your cool, Toby." Dax held his hand out in front of Toby. He couldn't let this get physical. "Chablis, go make sure Zinfandel is with TJ and don't let them come out here until I get you."

Brooks hadn't done anything illegal that Carter or the cops could find. It had all been Serena and her mother. Brooks had only been along for the ride, except for what he'd dug up on Dax, but that had all been partially true.

"Keep on walking," Dax said. "You're not welcome here."

"As soon as I find Serena, I'll be on my way." Brooks ran a hand through his shoulder-length hair. "She wasn't at TJ's game."

Toby took a step forward.

Dax inched between the two men.

Brooks laughed. "Relax. I don't want to be the kid's father. I just want the coaching job and I want to see Dax here fall off his high horse. I know Toby does too, so don't worry. TJ won't get hurt."

Toby shoved Dax to the side. "You stupid fuck. He already has because his mother was arrested."

"What the hell are you talking about?" Brooks jerked his head back.

Toby cocked his arm.

Dax grabbed Toby and yanked him two steps back. "Brooks, if you know what's best for you, you'll walk out of this rink and not come back. Let your assistant coaches step up the rest of the week. Consider yourself lucky that the cops haven't been able to find anything on you because your girlfriend is facing fifteen years in prison."

"That's bullshit." Brooks pulled his cell out of his pocket and stared at it for a long moment while he scratched the side of his face. "One of these days, Dax. One of these days." Brooks took off out the front door like he was running a marathon.

Toby shook out his hands. "I wanted to punch that asshole in the face."

"You and me both, man." Dax let out a long breath.

"I can't thank you enough for what you just did. I could have ended up in a cell next to Serena and that wouldn't have helped my son."

"What are friends for." Dax smiled. "Oh, wait. Can I call you that now?"

Toby slapped Dax on the back. "We might have crossed over into the friend zone." He rolled his neck. "I better go grab TJ and Zinfandel. This is going to be a hell of a week. I don't know what this is going to do to TJ's tryouts."

"Don't worry about it. He's got a spot on my team. I'll put the offer in writing today."

Toby blinked. "Seriously?"

"He's got some work. And if he's selfish on the ice, or you act like a jerk in the stands, he's sitting the bench, but yeah. I want him to be part of the CFW Prep hockey program."

"If you need a manager, I'd be happy to take the job." Toby smiled.

"Wow. Imagine you and me working together." Perhaps Weezer was right. Life did always come full circle.

15

CHABLIS

Chablis sat on the front porch of her family home, sipping a glass of her family's white wine. Nothing like a nice Sunday dinner when everyone in the entire family could be there. Even sweeter was her father decided to invite Toby and TJ. While Serena had been released on bail, a judge had granted Toby temporary physical custody until after the trial. If there was one. Her father hoped she took a plea deal, but thus far no one knew what her plans were. Toby's focus was on his son.

Dax stepped from the house and sat on the step next to her, his knee pressing against hers intimately. She'd waited a lifetime to be at this moment. She'd endured pain and sorrow and yet she wouldn't change anything about her life. They both could look back on their lives without regrets.

And move forward with a new chapter.

A life together.

One they shared.

"Hey, hot stuff," he said as he gave her a little nudge. "What are you doing out here?"

"Just watching Toby and Zinfandel play a little catch with TJ and wondering how Mother is handling this insane crush my sister has on Toby."

"I think you need to be more concerned with your dad," Dax said. "When I was in the kitchen getting a drink, he mentioned if he'd known, he might have only invited TJ, and Toby better not return the feelings."

Chablis watched as Zinfandel took the ball from Toby's hands and took off laughing. Toby ran off after her and TJ raised his arms and shook his head in what appears to be frustration. "Age is just a number when it comes to love."

"You're telling me you'd be okay with Toby dating your baby sister?" Dax said with an arched brow.

"It's not for me to decide what is right; as long as he treats my sister good, I've got no problem with it."

Dax took her chin with his thumb and forefinger. "You are one special lady. I love you, Chablis River."

"I love you right back, Dax Fabian."

He took her mouth passionately. Her mother once told her she would know a man loved her by the way he kissed.

And Dax kissed her like she was the only one who mattered.

. . .

Thank you for taking the time to read *Its In His Kiss*. Please feel free to leave an honest review. Next in the series is: *Lips Of An Angel*. And please check out the rest of the series:

Kisses Sweeter than Wine
A Little Bit Whiskey

Grab a glass of vino, kick back, relax, and let the romance roll in...
Sign up for my Newsletter (https://dl.bookfunnel.com/82gm8b9k4y) where I often give away free books before publication.

Join my private Facebook group (https://www.facebook.com/groups/191706547909047/) where I post exclusive excerpts and discuss all things murder and love!

READY FOR ANOTHER TRIP TO CANDLEWOOD FALLS?

For more Alpachino the Alpaca antics and to find out who went to prison for killing Sam's Father's read <u>TAKING ROOT</u> by Stacey Wilk.

And the second book in Stacey's series…What will Brad Wilde the man who has it all do when an orphan is dropped on his doorstep? RAISING WINTER by Stacey Wilk.

Also by Stacey Wilk in this series: Even the most unexpected circumstances may teach us how to forgive what cannot be changed. DEFINING CHANCES.

And While packing away her mothers life, Petra Wilde discovers a life of her own in BEGINNING OVER.

If you want to spend some time with Sam Wilde and his quest for an apple to make you happy and horny you'll want to read WILDE TEMPTATION by K.M. FAWCETT.

And the second book in K.M. Fawcett's series…Spend the holidays with Lacey Wilde, her dog Remi, and a sexy marine who claims Remi belongs to him in <u>WILDE CHRISTMAS</u> by K.M. Fawcett.

Also by K.M. Fawcett is WILD IN LOVE: Can a bad boy and a good girl overcome their fears to find true love?

And in WILDE TREASURES: While searching for a hidden fortune, can two lonely adventurers discover some treasurers are more precious than gold.

ACKNOWLEDGMENTS

A big thank you to Stacey Wilk and K.M. Fawcett for inviting me into Candlewood Falls.

ABOUT THE AUTHOR

Jen Talty is the *USA Today* Bestselling Author of Contemporary Romance, Romantic Suspense, and Paranormal Romance. In the fall of 2020, her short story was selected and featured in a 1001 Dark Nights Anthology.

Regardless of the genre, her goal is to take you on a ride that will leave you floating under the sun with warmth in your heart. She writes stories about broken heroes and heroines who aren't necessarily looking for romance, but in the end, they find the kind of love books are written about :).

She first started writing while carting her kids to one hockey rink after the other, averaging 170 games per year between 3 kids in 2 countries and 5 states. Her first book, IN TWO WEEKS was originally published in 2007. In 2010 she helped form a publishing company (Cool Gus Publishing) with *NY Times* Bestselling Author Bob Mayer where she ran the technical side of the business through 2016.

Jen is currently enjoying the next phase of her life...the empty nester! She and her husband reside in Jupiter, Florida.

Grab a glass of vino, kick back, relax, and let the romance roll in...

Sign up for my Newsletter (https://dl.bookfunnel.com/82gm8b9k4y) *where I often give away free books before publication.*

Join my private Facebook group *(https://www.facebook.com/groups/191706547909047/) where I post exclusive excerpts and discuss all things murder and love!*

Never miss a new release. Follow me on Amazon:amazon.com/author/jentalty

And on Bookbub: bookbub.com/authors/jen-talty

ALSO BY JEN TALTY

Everyone needs a SAFE HARBOR!

Mine To Keep

Mine To Save

Mine To Protect

Mine to Hold

Mine to Love

Check out LOVE IN THE ADIRONDACKS!

Shattered Dreams

An Inconvenient Flame

The Wedding Driver

Clear Blue Sky

Blue Moon

Before the Storm

NY STATE TROOPER SERIES (also set in the Adirondacks!)

In Two Weeks

Dark Water

Deadly Secrets

Murder in Paradise Bay

To Protect His own

Deadly Seduction

When A Stranger Calls

His Deadly Past

The Corkscrew Killer

First Responders: A spin-off from the NY State Troopers series

Playing With Fire

Private Conversation

The Right Groom

After The Fire

Caught In The Flames

Chasing The Fire

Legacy Series

Dark Legacy

Legacy of Lies

Secret Legacy

Emerald City

Investigate Away

Sail Away

Fly Away

Flirt Away

Hawaii Brotherhood Protectors

Waylen Unleashed

Bowie's Battle

Colorado Brotherhood Protectors

Fighting For Esme

Defending Raven

Fay's Six

Darius' Promise

Yellowstone Brotherhood Protectors

Guarding Payton

Wyatt's Mission

Corbin's Mission

Candlewood Falls

Rivers Edge

The Buried Secret

Its In His Kiss

Lips Of An Angel

Kisses Sweeter than Wine

A Little Bit Whiskey

It's all in the Whiskey

Johnnie Walker

Georgia Moon

Jack Daniels

Jim Beam

Whiskey Sour

Whiskey Cobbler

Whiskey Smash

Irish Whiskey

The Monroes

Color Me Yours

Color Me Smart

Color Me Free

Color Me Lucky

Color Me Ice

Color Me Home

Search and Rescue

Protecting Ainsley

Protecting Clover

Protecting Olympia

Protecting Freedom

Protecting Princess

Protecting Marlowe

Fallport Rescue Operations

Searching for Madison

Searching for Haven

Searching for Pandora

Searching for Stormi

DELTA FORCE-NEXT GENERATION

Shielding Jolene

Shielding Aalyiah

Shielding Laine

Shielding Talullah

Shielding Maribel

Shielding Daisy

The Men of Thief Lake

Rekindled

Destiny's Dream

Federal Investigators

Jane Doe's Return

The Butterfly Murders

THE AEGIS NETWORK

The Sarich Brother

The Lighthouse

Her Last Hope

The Last Flight

The Return Home

The Matriarch

Aegis Network: Jacksonville Division

A SEAL's Honor

Talon's Honor

Arthur's Honor

Rex's Honor

Kent's Honor

Buddy's Honor

Aegis Network Short Stories

Max & Milian

A Christmas Miracle

Spinning Wheels

Holiday's Vacation

The Brotherhood Protectors

Out of the Wild

Rough Justice

Rough Around The Edges

Rough Ride

Rough Edge

Rough Beauty

The Brotherhood Protectors

The Saving Series

Saving Love

Saving Magnolia

Saving Leather

Hot Hunks

Cove's Blind Date Blows Up

My Everyday Hero – Ledger

Tempting Tavor

Malachi's Mystic Assignment

Needing Neor

Holiday Romances

A Christmas Getaway

Alaskan Christmas

Whispers

Christmas In The Sand

Heroes & Heroines on the Field

Taking A Risk

Tee Time

A New Dawn

The Blind Date

Spring Fling

Summers Gone

Winter Wedding

The Awakening

Fated Moons

The Collective Order

The Lost Sister

The Lost Soldier

The Lost Soul

The Lost Connection

The New Order